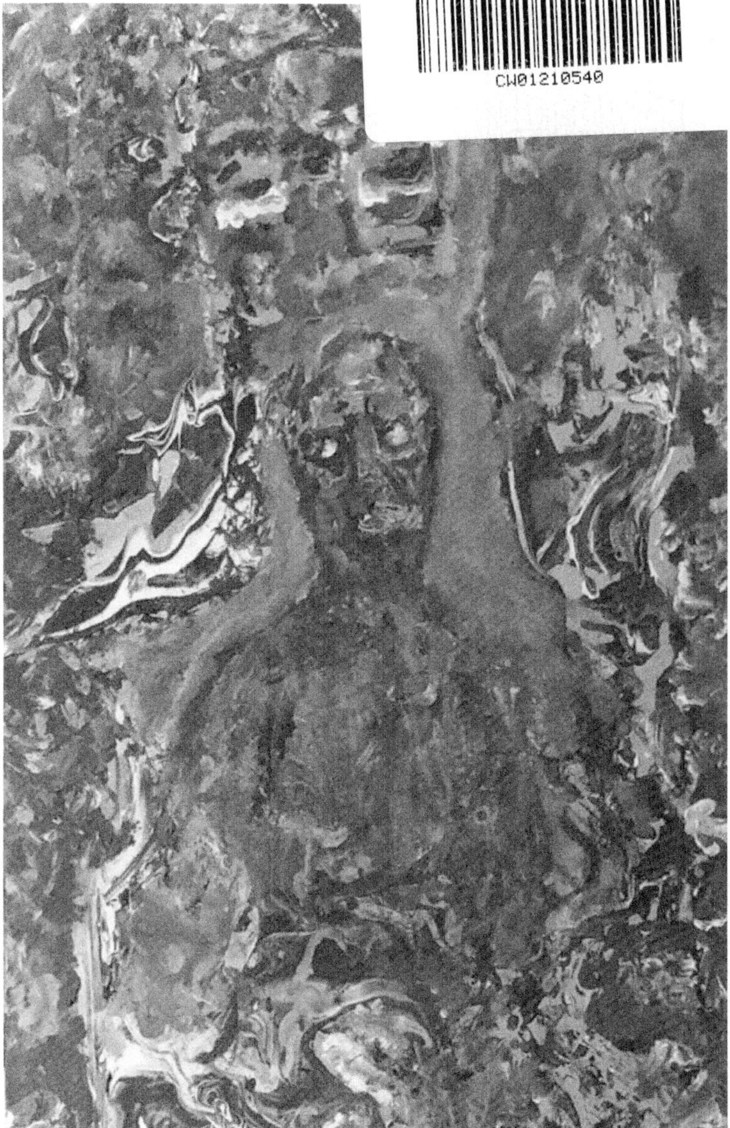

All the best
Martin

This book is dedicated to the memory of

Nigel Richards.

One of the kindest souls to ever grace this world.

One of my most dedicated and loyal readers and advocates.

You were more than just my cousin,

you were my friend.

I have tears in my eyes as I write this.

I shall miss you enormously.

I would also like to add another dedication to

Rosie May Rickards

A true warrior who fought bravely until the end

And always wore a smile on her face

May you both rest in peace

Portal. A story by Martin McGregor

This book was first published in the UK in 2022 by Marlebond Publishing.

ISBN: 9798801220055

Copyright © Martin McGregor 2022.

He has asserted the right of Martin McGregor to be identified as the author of this work under the copyright, Designs and Patents Act 1988.

All rights reserved. No part of this publication may be reproduced, stored in or introduced into a retrieval system, or transmitted in any form, or by any means (electronic, mechanical, photocopying, recording or otherwise) without the publisher's prior written permission. Any person who does any unauthorised act concerning this publication may be liable to criminal prosecution and civil claim damages.

This story is a work of fiction. Names, characters, businesses, places, events and incidents are either the products of the author's imagination or used in a purely fictitious manner. Any resemblance to actual persons, living or dead, or any real events, is purely coincidental.

Original cover design by Gareth Jones

Instagram @g_manwoohoo

This book is sold subject to the conditions that it shall not, by way of trade or other means, be lent, re-sold, hired out or otherwise circulated without the publisher's prior consent in any form of binding or cover other than that in which it is published and without a similar condition including this condition being imposed on the subsequent purchaser.

While Marlebond Publishing makes every effort to see that no inaccurate or misleading data, opinion or statement appears in this book or any other affiliated publications, Marlebond Publishing wishes to state that the data in this book and other related publications are the responsibility of the author concerned. Marlebond Publishing and their officers and agents A whatsoever for the consequences of any such misleading data, opinion, or statement.

Marlebond
Publishing

Also available from this author:

Ellie Caitlin the complete collection

Keep away from the windows

Keep away from the windows 2: The dark ones

Keep away from the windows 3: The world in my eyes

Damaged Goods

24

24: The return

Exit 12

24: The end times

Atlanta Rain

Absolution

Atlanta Rain: Into the Inferno

Atlanta Rain: The Nine Realms

Slide

The Lost Girls

The Hunger Inside

Distorted Visions

Distorted Visions: The Killing Jar

Distorted Visions: Insomnia

Distorted Visions: The Heart of Twilight

The Order

Introduction

I have to confess that Portal is a bit of an oddity for me, in that I don't normally know where my stories originate from (aside from my messed up imagination). This book was inspired by the incredible painting featured on the cover, used with the artist's kind permission, my friend Gareth Jones. The very moment that I viewed the painting, it conjured up a dark image of a soul trapped in torment behind the canvas and from that vision, this story was born.

Despite a turbocharged beginning, the story took a long time to formulate as I wanted to do the image justice. This book has taken around six months to complete. It feels good to return to my horror roots, and I already have an exciting idea for the next novel. I hope that you enjoy the book, and you can follow me on Twitter @MartinMcGregorHorrorAuthor or Facebook@Martin Mcgregor Author Fanpage. Enjoy!

Martin

Thank you to the following people.

Heather and Sean Swinson for all of your never-ending help and support. You are appreciated! My mother Brenda. My sons, Nick, Chris, Jordan and Owen. My grandchildren, Freddie, Bobby, Marley, Dahlia and Ace for all of the joy you give me. To Tracey Elena, for your support and encouragement and for sharing my madness.

To my readers, including Jennifer Bastholm, Denise Patient, Jazz Sawyer, Judith Monk, Tracey Ware, Andy Turner, Ali and Mark Gibbs, Maurice Sweeney, Steve Bodsworth, Maggi and Andrew and to all of my readers who enjoy sharing the madness. My heartfelt thanks go out to you all.

Now let's open up a portal to another realm where art truly imitates life.

Enjoy!

Youth knows no pain

Ingrid groaned out loud as she held on to the dining table for support while rising from her chair. There was a creaking sound as she stood upright. and she would always joke with her granddaughter, Louhi that she was unsure if it was the chair that creaked, or if it had been her ageing bones. Her birthday was coming up soon, in May she would reach the landmark age of seventy years old. The thought of reaching seventy was terrifying to her. The cold weather here in Lapland where they lived did her aching joints no favours, but she had no choice but to get up and walk.

Her granddaughter Louhi was going to be late for work and that was not like her at all. Ingrid groaned as she started the long walk down the hallway towards Louhi's bedroom. She had been caring for her granddaughter since Louhi was twelve years old. That was the year when Louhi's mother had been killed by a drunk driver while she was on her way home from work. The driver had fled the scene without alerting the emergency services, and her body lay hidden in a ditch by the side of the road. It was another eleven hours before she was found, and when they had discovered her body, it was frozen to the ground beneath her. Louhi's father had disappeared before she had reached her first birthday, and no one had heard anything from him since.

It wasn't normal for Louhi to get up late in the morning. She was a good girl who helped out around the house. Louhi also worked as a cleaner for a local supermarket, giving almost all of the money she earned to her grandmother to help with food and the household bills. Louhi had just turned nineteen, and she was the mirror image of her mother. She was very good looking, and her grandmother did everything that she could to keep her away from the sexually charged males in the local village, but there had been a few near misses in the past.

Ingrid tapped on the bedroom door and waited for a few seconds before tapping on the door again just a little louder. She was met with silence.

"Louhi, you are going to be late for work. You must get up!" She shouted, but there was still no response.

Ingrid opened the bedroom door and placed her head inside the room. The bedroom was colder than usual. The window was open, and it looked as if Louhi's bed had not been slept in. As she looked around the bedroom, there was a note on the dressing table with Ingrid's name written on the front of it. The grandmother felt uneasy as she walked across the room and picked up the envelope, opened it carefully and then began to read its contents.

My Dearest Grandmother,

I have been offered an opportunity to leave this place, and to become a glamour model. I have been told that in England, I can make more money than we could ever dream of. and I have decided to try and make a better life for myself. I am travelling to another country with my boyfriend where I have been promised that he will look after me. He will be my manager and show me how to build a decent career. I promise that I will send your money home and will come to visit you as often as I can. I am sorry that I did not tell you earlier, but I did not want you to try and change my mind. Please do not worry. I will be in safe hands and I promise you that I will call you as soon as I reach England.

All of my love,

Louhi x

Ingrid lowered her hands with the letter still held tightly between her fingers. Louhi had no passport, and as far as Ingrid had known, she did not have a boyfriend either. A sense of dread washed over her, and she feared the worst for her granddaughter. She dropped the letter on the bed, and then she began to search through the bedroom for any clues as to what had been going on behind her back. As she trawled through the drawers and cupboards, it looked as if just a few items of clothing were missing.

When Ingrid looked underneath the mattress, she discovered some instant pictures where Louhi was posing like a model while in various states of undress, and the lewdness of the content in some of the pictures shocked her. Ingrid was confident that her granddaughter had been drawn away from the country under false pretences. Louhi had never ventured outside of the village of Autti before, let alone the country.

Ingrid swore out loud that if any harm came to her last living descendant, then she would curse whoever laid a finger on her, to an eternity of pain as they burned in the fires of hell. Despite her age and waning memory, she still had the legacy left to her by her ancestors and she had the power to make the curse real.

Invisible

Gareth awoke in a daze and he blinked repeatedly as he opened up his eyes to see the bright light that was flooding in from the open gap in the curtains that were hanging over the bedroom window. His head was pounding hard as if he had been kicked about both of his temples by a small army while he had slept. His mouth felt really dry and despite his initial confusion, he soon realised that he was suffering from having drunk too much.

Usually, Gareth would try and sleep off a hangover, but his throat was sore this morning and would soon need to rehydrate. Although he still felt tired, he was thirsty enough to make an effort to get out of bed and make his way out to the kitchen for a glass of water. He groaned loudly as he lifted the duvet off of his body and reluctantly dangled both feet over the edge of the mattress. It was cold enough in the bedroom to make the hairs on his arms stand up, and it made his body shudder.

Gareth started to cough hoarsely. He had given up smoking over a year ago, but he could taste whiskey and smell the scent of cigarettes from somewhere in the bedroom this morning. That horrid smell of nicotine had stuck to his discarded clothes that now lay strewn all over the floor next to his bed. He knew that he must have been quite close to smokers in a communal area at some point, and even from here, he could smell that the clothes stank of second-hand smoke and the smell was so bad, that it made him feel sick.

The boxer shorts that he had worn the night before were on the floor next to the bed and he pulled them on, and then he heard the sound of a loud moan coming from underneath the thick duvet that was now doubled over on the other side of the bed. The noise startled him. The moaning sound was unmistakably coming from a female, but Gareth had no idea who it was that was sleeping in his bed.

As the full force of his hangover kicked in at precisely the wrong moment, he realised that the bedroom also smelled of sex as well as cigarettes and he felt even more confused and slightly panicked. Gareth wracked his brains to try and remember anything at all from the previous night, and more importantly if he could just remember the name of the woman who had just spent the night with him. One thing was for certain, he knew that it wasn't his wife who was asleep in the bed.

Gareth's wife Natalie was still in France on business and he knew that she wasn't due to return home again for another two weeks. He rubbed both of his temples firmly with his fingers, desperately to remember anything at all, but the gentle massage from his fingers wasn't helping. His mind was still drawing a total blank.

As he left the bedroom Gareth felt a little light-headed as he walked out into the kitchen. He reached up into the cupboard to the left of the sink, and in a daze, he took out a pint glass from the upper shelf and closed the door behind him. The glass was relatively clean, but a little dusty from a lack of use. He turned on the cold water tap, rinsed out the glass and then he poured himself a pint of water. The water looked cloudy inside of the glass, and after taking just a small mouthful, he spat the water back down into the sink. The tap was still running, and there was no bottled water in the house, so he waited until the water had run for a little longer, and then he emptied his glass into the sink and filled it up again with some much colder water.

The glass felt cold to the touch and holding the glass up in front of his face, he could see that the water looked to be much clearer too. Gareth noticed that his right hand was trembling slightly and he knew that he needed to cut down on the amount of alcohol he was consuming. He moved the glass to his lips and he drank over half of the pint down in one go. The water still tasted horrible, but it was cold, and it soothed his throat so he would just have to live with it.

His thoughts then turned back to his hangover as the pain in his temples seemed to amplify tenfold. All of the medicine within the flat was stored safely up high in the bathroom cabinet away from any visitor's young children, so begrudgingly he made his way out to the bathroom shuffling his feet along the wooden floor to try and find some paracetamol to help his hangover.

Gareth opened both of the mirrored glass doors of the cabinet, and he shifted the various boxes of medicine around inside until he found the box of pills that he had been looking for. He ripped open the blue and white coloured box and popped two of the tablets out from the strip. After throwing the pills into his mouth, he used the remainder of the water from his glass to swallow the tablets and then he placed the medicine box back on the shelf and closed the cabinet door after him.

He jumped up and almost screamed out in fright as he saw the pale face of a stranger staring at him in the mirror. The woman had come from out of nowhere and she was now silently standing behind him in the bathroom.

The glass dropped from Gareth's hand and fell into the enamel sink where it smashed into numerous pieces.

"Fuck!" Gareth shouted as he gathered his breath. He had not heard the woman enter the bathroom behind him and she was now standing in front of him completely naked, and without any hint of embarrassment at her state of undress.

"I know I'm probably not looking my best this morning, but I didn't think that I looked as bad as that!" The woman joked. She had what sounded like a European twang to her accent, but Gareth had never heard an accent like it, nor had he seen her before.

"I'm so sorry, I didn't hear you walk into the bathroom, and you scared the life out of me."

"Sorry." She said apologetically, and she stared upward at Gareth as he looked over her naked body.

Although he felt uneasy, Gareth was a little impressed by the fact that he had managed to end up with such a good looking woman in his bed, and his friends would have all been happy to cover things up for him without actively encouraging him to cheat on his wife. No doubt the copious amounts of bourbon he had consumed had given his confidence a much-needed boost, but now he began to feel some serious pangs of guilt about having cheated on his wife.

He tried to justify what he had done by telling himself that he was a male who had natural urges and his wife was always going away on business, so it had been a few weeks since he had last had any female company in the bedroom. He just wished that he could remember the woman's bloody name and then he might not feel so embarrassed.

The woman had faded scars that were dotted all over her body, and he quickly realised that she was staring up at him in silence as he surveyed the entirety of her naked form.

"How's your head this morning?" Gareth asked, just trying to make polite conversation and to distract her from his peering looks at her body.

"It's fine, but if you don't mind I do need to take a pee."

Gareth's face went bright red as he suddenly realised why the woman had been staring at him blankly for the last few minutes, as he had been standing right in front of the toilet while she was waiting to use it.

"Yes, of course, you can. I'm so sorry. I'm an idiot. Just let me clean up this broken glass from the sink for you first." He offered.

"It's fine, I will do it for you after I have used the toilet. I can't hold on much longer." She pleaded as she crossed her legs in front of him.

"Fuck! I'm so sorry I'm going to let you go." He replied light-heartedly, Gareth was shaking his head in disbelief at how confused he was this morning, and he felt the need to explain. "I must have drunk too much last night and I am hanging out of my arse this morning. Let me get out of the bathroom so you can use the toilet." Gareth brushed against the woman's naked body as he squeezed past her and exited the bathroom.

For some unknown reason, Gareth turned around and met the woman's gaze just as she was closing the bathroom door behind him.

"Thank you for being so kind." She said, and she smiled at him before she closed and locked the heavy wooden door.

Gareth had smiled at the girl before he had turned away from her.

"Weird" Gareth said as he mumbled under his breath while he walked off down the hallway. He had no idea what act of kindness it was that the woman was referring to.

As Gareth walked back into the bedroom, he gathered up the rest of his clothes from the night before. He was going to need a shower, and then afterwards he would offer to drive the woman home before the nosy neighbours noticed that he had female company in the flat. Given the circumstances of her overnight stay, it was the least he could do for her.

He walked through the hallway into the living room throwing his dirty clothes on the sofa because he hadn't emptied the washing machine yet, and then he carried on out into the kitchen. He emptied the old water kettle and filled it with fresh water from the tap, turned the power button on and then sat down at the breakfast bar. He could hear the sound of the toilet flushing, and then oddly, he could hear the sound of water running in the bath.

His unexpected guest seemed to be making full use of the amenities on offer, but he couldn't complain, as he imagined that he had used her body just to fulfil his sexual urges, much to his shame. Now he couldn't even remember where he had met the girl. He was still trying desperately to recall anything from the previous night's escapades, and this episode of hungover short term memory loss was far worse than usual.

Gareth could remember being in a pub and singing a Duran Duran song on the karaoke around ten, but then things started to get a little bit blurry afterwards. The kettle whistle sounded and Gareth was snapped out of his train of thought as the appliance screamed out at him from across the kitchen. He jumped up from the chair and turned off the kettle before making himself a strong cup of coffee, adding in an extra spoon of sugar for a quick burst of energy.

After throwing his dirty spoon into the dishwasher, he thought about emptying the washing machine but felt tired, so he decided against it, and walked out of the kitchen, through the living room, and out into his conservatory at the rear of the flat that now doubled up as the couple's art studio. The room was originally designed to be a laundry room, but the couple had always referred to it as 'the conservatory' as it sounded a little more luxurious.

The art studio had come about after Gareth had a nasty ski accident. He had broken his leg in four places whilst holidaying in Bulgaria some eighteen months ago. After the couple returned to England, he had become pretty much housebound for a few months, and he soon grew bored with the daytime television programmes. During those long months, he had decided to find a new hobby to stop him from going stir crazy.

After trying out his hand at various subjects, and after a great deal of encouragement from his wife, Gareth had discovered that he quite enjoyed painting to the point where he soon found it very therapeutic.

There was a relatively new painting on a large canvas hanging on the wall. It was a picture of the view across Andover as seen from the conservatory. The focal point was the town church that was called St. Mary's Church. Gareth had struggled to capture the feel of the heart of the town, and as he stared across at the picture, he was disappointed with the final image that he had painted. His wife seemed to love it though.

After slowly finishing off his cup of coffee, tiredness washed over him, and he closed his eyes for just a few moments. He later awoke with a start and checked his watch. It was almost midday. He had no idea how long he had been asleep, but it felt as if his guest had been in the bathroom for quite a long time. Gareth then began to worry that even though it was highly unlikely, for some reason, his wife might have decided to surprise him and unexpectedly arrived home early. She had surprised him a few times in the past before.

Not willing to risk the chance and having to explain himself, he decided to try and hurry his guest along just in case. Once the woman was gone, then he could change the bedsheets and then settle down to watch the football later in the day. There was a Liverpool football match on later, and he loved to watch them play while partaking in a few cold beers with the lads who would always come around to his flat, purely because his television was huge, and they knew that his fridge was always regularly filled up with beer.

After placing the empty coffee mug in the dishwasher tray, Gareth popped a tablet into the holder and closed the appliance door. Despite the machine being less than half full, he was running out of mugs and cutlery (as was usually the case when Natalie was away). He turned the machine on and walked out into the hallway. He was still wearing nothing other than his boxer shorts. Oddly, he could hear that inside the bathroom, the taps were still running, and he reasoned that the bath must have surely been filled up by now?

"Are you alright in there?" He shouted at the door, but there was no response from the woman inside.

Gareth was worried that his guest may have fallen asleep in the bath, so he tapped hard on the door with his knuckles to try and wake her. "Hello?" He shouted a few times, but still, there was no response from her.

There was a warm feeling around Gareth's feet, and he turned the hallway light on. As the hallway became brighter, Gareth gasped out loud as he slipped and fell backwards to the floor on the water that was flooding out from underneath the bathroom door and soaking into the laminate flooring. Gareth cursed out loud at his clumsiness as he sat upright, and then he noticed that the water looked a strange colour, and suddenly he realised why. There was blood in the water, and not just a small amount of blood either. The woman in the bathroom had to be in some serious trouble.

After jumping up to his feet, Gareth tried the bathroom door handle. The door was still locked from the inside. He decided to bust the lock open by barging into the door with his shoulder. It took three attempts, but eventually, he applied enough force with using his body weight that the door opened inwards, and he almost fell headfirst into the toilet bowl as he stumbled inside of the room. Then he saw the woman lying motionless in the bathtub, and suddenly he felt faint and sick to the stomach.

"No, no no!" He said out loud to himself as he entered into a state of sheer panic.

The bath was overflowing, and the bloody water continued to run over the side. Underneath the water, the young woman's face looked deathly pale, and her lips had turned blue. Long gashes were ripped deep into the flesh along both of her arms, and there was a large piece of the broken pint glass which was covered in blood that was just laying on top of the bathmat next to the bath.

The woman had slashed both of her wrists so deeply, that she had lost a large amount of blood in just a short space of time. Gareth knew from basic first aid, that he had to stop the bleeding and to do that, pressure had to be applied to a wound, but he couldn't apply pressure to both of her arms, and he was afraid that the woman was already dead. He was in a very bad place, and he had no idea what he should do next.

Drowning man

With its sirens blaring, and blue lights flashing, an ambulance was quickly dispatched to the scene, with a police car following closely behind it. Both vehicles had arrived at the flat around forty minutes after Gareth had made the emergency telephone call, and despite the paramedics doing everything that they possibly could to save her, the young woman was pronounced dead soon after the ambulance had arrived. The flat was quickly cordoned off and then Gareth had been escorted down the stairs and taken away in the back of a police car.

Gareth felt numb. He was now sitting in the police station wearing just a pair of jeans and a t-shirt. They were clothes that he had worn the night before after picking them up from the sofa. They had never made it into the washing machine after all and they still stank of stale smoke. His mind was all over the place, and he was unable to even think straight. The dirty clothes were the first things that he threw on, despite having clean clothes in the living room and they made him want to retch. He had agreed to give a statement, but in his head, he remained confused by what had happened, he was still desperate to recall anything that had happened the night before. Everything was already a blur, and the events of the morning had only compounded his confusion even further.

A female C.I.D officer soon entered the interview room. She was carrying a notepad in her hands along with a hot cup of coffee. She looked to be in her late thirties or early forties. Her blonde hair was cut into a short bob, and she was wearing a two-piece grey suit that made her look a little older than her years. The officer closed the door of the interview room by pushing it using her foot and then her backside and then she turned to face Gareth.

The officer's face was stony, and her tone was harsh.

"Are you sure you don't want a coffee or anything?" She asked. Gareth shook his head from side to side. He had been asked the same question three times already since arriving here, and each time he had said no. He was happy enough with the never-ending supply of water from the jug using the plastic cup that they had given him. His body still felt dehydrated from the night before, no matter how much he drank.

"I'm fine. I just want to answer whatever questions you have for me and to get out of here as soon as possible." He replied.

The officer placed her items on the desk in front of her. She pulled out the chair and sat down directly opposite where Gareth was sitting.

"Alright then, let's begin. My name is officer Denise Cole. I know that you've experienced a traumatic event this morning, but I need to go over what happened at your flat earlier today. Before we begin, I just wanted to let you know that I will be recording this conversation. Do you have any objections to that?" Gareth looked up at her momentarily.

"Would it matter if I did?"

"In all honesty, no. It wouldn't" There was a certain degree of animosity in her voice that Gareth felt was unwarranted.

"Then why don't you just go ahead. I don't have anything to hide from you." He told her, shrugging his shoulders nonchalantly as he did so.

Officer Cole broke out a new cassette tape from its plastic packaging, and after opening the inner case, she removed the tape from inside and wrote something on the white paper stripe on the front of it and placed the blank tape into a machine.

"I thought those things had been retired a long time ago," Gareth said, and he smiled at her trying to show her that he was friendly.

"I will retire before this thing does." She replied. At first, he thought that the officer was joking, but her face was rigid, and her tone remained serious. "Interview with the detainee named Gareth Chambers, also present in the room is me, and my name for the record is Officer Denise Cole. You don't have to say anything, but what you do say may be used in court. Alright Gareth, would you tell me in your own words what happened to the young woman in your flat earlier this morning?"

Gareth took a deep sigh before he began to speak. He wanted to cover everything that happened and be as clear and concise as possible.

"As I told the officers who came to my flat earlier. I went out on the town with some friends last night. I got very drunk and I honestly can't remember what happened. I must have met the woman at some point during the evening and the next thing I knew, I woke up this morning and I found her in the flat. She was asleep in my bed."

"Thank you. Can you tell me, what was the woman's name Gareth?" The officers' tone had darkened somewhat. She sounded like she was becoming angry with him for some unknown reason.

"I don't know her name. Look, how many more times do I have to say the same thing? I woke up. I was hanging out of my arse and there she was, laid in my bed. Surely you must have checked to see if she had had some form of identification with her. The clothes that she was wearing, they had to still be in the bedroom on the floor somewhere. Did you check inside of them for what you need?"

"Oh, we already found her clothes in your room, but she had nothing in them that we could use to identify her. She was carrying no money about her person, she had no bag or purse, and she had no bank cards with her. At this moment in time, we have no idea who she is, and we have no fingerprint matches for her in our database. Even dental records aren't showing any matches. That is highly unusual wouldn't you say?"

"Is it? I guess so. You tell me, you are the ones who are paid to investigate! I..."

Gareth quickly realised that his tone was becoming far too aggressive, and it might paint him in a different light, so he decided to stop talking before he made things worse for himself. He was starting to wonder if he might be needing a solicitor soon, but he brushed the thought aside. He hadn't done anything wrong, so he had nothing to worry about. Or did he?

Denise leant forward on the desk and placed her chin down on top of her interlocked fingers, with her elbows spread wide apart on the table. She looked like she was pleased with herself after hearing Gareth's sudden outburst, and now she had a smug grin etched right across her face.

"So, can you tell me how it is that a woman you only met the night before was found dead in your bath?" Gareth was sure that the officer was smiling at him. He couldn't disguise his frustration anymore.

"For fucks sake, here we go again!" Despite his best efforts to control himself, he couldn't help himself and the angry response came flooding out of his mouth.

His anger was now evident for all to hear as he raised his voice to another level. "I told you, my head was fucking pounding, so I got up out of bed and I went to get a drink of water. She was still in the bedroom at that point. Right? I took the glass of water with me into the bathroom, and I looked in the cabinet where I found some paracetamol for my headache. I never heard her come into the bathroom at all.

She crept up behind me and when I looked in the mirror, she was there, and it startled me. I dropped the glass, and it smashed to pieces in the sink. The woman told me that she needed the toilet and that she would clean up the broken glass, so I left her in the bathroom. I went to the kitchen and made myself a coffee and sat down in the conservatory. I heard the toilet flush and the sound of her running a bath. Then I dozed off for a short while. Okay?" He slumped back in his chair with his hands placed behind his head and stared up at the ceiling.

"It's very convenient that you fell asleep. Can I ask are you always in the habit of letting unknown women take a bath in your flat while your wife is away?" Gareth paused before he replied. What the fuck did she mean by that he wondered?

Before Gareth even had time to answer the officer, Denise began to ask him another question. "Just how long was she in the bathroom before you decided to go and check on her?" Gareth thought carefully before he replied. He could feel his pulse racing through the veins in his neck and he was trying to calm himself down. He paused for a few seconds to catch his breath and when he felt calm enough, he answered the question.

"I can't have been asleep for very long, so it must have been around half an hour or so. I guess."

"It must have been a rather large mug of coffee that you were drinking?" She questioned and Gareth struggled to hold back. He could see that smug shit-eating grin appearing on her face again.

"No. I was daydreaming in the art studio, and I was trying to remember her name. It was embarrassing that I couldn't recall who she was. Then I fell asleep."

"And when you finally decided that you needed to check on her Gareth, tell me what happened then?"

Gareth now had to focus hard on how he replied. He wasn't sure where these questions were going, but he didn't appreciate the tone that the officer was using, and he didn't want to incriminate himself in any way.

"I noticed there was water on the hallway floor, and then I realised that there was blood in it, so I broke the door down. Once I was inside the bathroom, I found the woman under the water in the bathtub, with her wrists slashed. She looked like she might be dead, but I wasn't sure. I pulled her up in the bath so that her head was above the water, and I wrapped her arms in towels as tightly as I could and then I ran for my phone, to call an ambulance."

"Did you have intercourse with her, and if so, at what point during the morning did you have sex with the woman?" Gareth was taken aback by the directness of the question he had just been asked.

"I think that I might have, but I don't remember. I honestly don't."

"At any point during the morning, did you fight with her, or did the sex become a little too aggressive? Did she say no to you, and did it make you angry that she was leading you on?" What the hell was she trying to say to him Gareth wondered.

"Not that I remember. What sort of question is that anyway? What are you accusing me of, what the fuck is going on here?" Gareth shouted. His face was turning red with anger.

"I can see that I have touched a nerve. Was that what happened earlier? Did she wind you up too, did she keep on pushing you until you snapped? It happens to us all sometimes."

"I didn't fucking hurt her! I tried to save her!" Gareth had heard enough. I don't know what you think I did, but I'm not saying anything more until I speak to a solicitor." He crossed his arms defensively and sat back in the chair staring up at the ceiling in defiance.

"Understood. The interview is suspended at 13.17 on the 12th of October 2021."

As Denise turned off the tape, Gareth leaned forward on the table. He was just about to speak when Denise asked him another question.

"Do you have a solicitor, or do you want to consult with the duty solicitor?" Gareth had never needed a criminal solicitor before, nor did he know any local ones.

"I don't have one. I need the duty solicitor." Denise was just about to stand up when Gareth looked her straight in the eyes.

"Now that the tape is off, can you tell me exactly what is it that you think I did to her?"

"The tape might be off, but if you look up at the ceiling behind you, you can see that you are still being recorded." She said, glancing up to the left-hand corner of the room behind Gareth.

There was a small camera pointing down into the room that he had not seen before. "I would advise you not to say anything more until your solicitor arrives." Gareth began to feel sick with worry. He felt like a drowning man out at sea without a float and the waves that he was riding on were getting rougher by the minute.

Is there something I should know?

Gareth's watch had been taken away from him by the desk sergeant on his arrival at the station, so it was difficult to tell how long it had been, but it felt like hours before the duty solicitor finally arrived. Up to that point, he had been locked in a cell and had paced backwards and forwards while trying to remember anything that had happened the night before. Frustratingly, his mind was still a total blank.

There had been far too many occasions in the past where he had lost a few hours while out drinking, but never to this extent, and always within a few hours of waking up, his embarrassing antics would have been remembered by him or sometimes they had been shared on social media by his friends. He wondered if it was the stress of the whole situation that was making him draw a blank now?

The small rectangular hatch squealed noisily as it was opened in the cell door, and an officer peered through into the cell.

"Your solicitor is here now. I need you to stand back from the door and I will let you out."

Gareth breathed a sigh of relief. He was starting to feel like this nightmare might soon be over, and he could return home to his flat. Then his thoughts went off on a different tangent. How long would it be before they released him, and he was allowed to return to his home? Would they have cleaned up the blood in the bathroom? How would he ever be able to use that bath again after what had happened?

The key turned and the cell door opened, and with the thought of his impending release being close, all those thoughts were temporarily lost.

"Step outside of the cell and turn to your right please." The officer instructed, and Gareth was only too happy to comply just to get out of the stuffy sterile cell.

The officer escorted him along the hallway to an interview room, where the duty solicitor was already waiting inside for him. He was dressed in a very expensive looking smart dark blue fitted suit, with a white shirt, and a light blue silk tie. As Gareth entered the room, the solicitor held out his right hand to greet him.

"Hello, nice to meet you. My name is Giles Morton. I have been appointed as your duty solicitor. You must be Gareth?" Gareth nodded toward him and shook his hand. The solicitor's handshake was weak, and that concerned him. His late father had once warned him to never trust a man with a weak handshake, and he had always found this piece of advice to be prudent over the years.

"Nice to meet you," Gareth replied.

The solicitor looked over towards the officer, who was still present in the room with them.

"I would like some time alone with my client now if you don't mind?" The officer nodded silently before walking back to the duty desk without saying another word.

Giles opened his smart black leather briefcase, and he took out some forms along with a pen and handed them over to Gareth.

"If you could just fill these in. They give me the power to act on your behalf. Please, take a seat." Giles offered. Gareth sat down, and after a cursory glance over the paperwork, he filled in everything that he could and signed the documents. He handed them back to Giles, who checked them over carefully before placing them back in his briefcase.

"What the hell is going on here?" Gareth asked him.

"I was rather hoping that you might be able to tell me that," Giles replied as he sat down opposite Gareth with his notepad held in his hand. He was waiting patiently to hear Gareth's version of the morning's awful tragedy.

Laughing Boy

Gareth relayed all that he could remember about the morning's unfortunate events to the solicitor, Giles took some notes down at regular intervals and when Gareth had finished telling him his version of what had occurred, Giles crossed his legs and he sat back in the chair. He looked completely relaxed, and comfortable as if he had been in this position hundreds of times before. Gareth wished that he had an ounce of his confidence right now, but the longer this saga went on, the more worried he felt about where all this was heading.

Giles smiled at him.

"Well, from what you have told me, they have no real reason to hold you any longer. They have to release you within twenty-four hours unless they apply for an extension, but I don't see any grounds for that to be granted. Now, I want you to listen to me carefully. In a few moments, I will call the investigating officer in. I want you to answer the questions they put to you honestly, and I will interject if I feel the need to stop you or add something. Are you okay with that?"

"Definitely. I just want this whole charade to be over with. I want to go home before my wife finds out about all of this." Gareth replied. Giles smirked as if he was dealing with a naughty schoolchild, and then he stood up and he peered around the edge of the door. He waved to the custody officer up the desk to try and attract his attention. It took the officer a few seconds before he finally looked up and noticed the solicitor.

"We are ready for the officers now," Giles shouted across to him.

"Alright, I will let them know." The desk sergeant picked up the telephone and made a call. It was at least another fifteen minutes before Denise had made her way back down to the interview room, and this time as she entered, she was not alone.

The two officers now entered the interview room and in turn, they both shook hands with the solicitor. It was clear that they knew each other well, and that there was a great deal of mutual respect between them. The four of them all took their seats.

"Are we ready to begin again?" Denise asked.

"My client is ready to answer your questions, happy to co-operate and desperate for a quick resolution to this unfortunate misunderstanding," Giles replied.

Denise pressed the record button down on the tape recorder.

"Interview re-commenced at fifteen hundred hours on the twelfth of October." She said, reading out the names of all four of those present including her fellow interviewing officer who went by the name of Nigel Baxter.

"Gareth, earlier today you told me about the events of this

morning, and how the as of yet unidentified female, came to be in your bathroom. I need to ask you again, did you have sex with the woman at any point in the last twenty-four hours?"

"I honestly don't remember."

"Oh, come on, a pretty young thing like that? That's one to brag about with the boys! Surely you would remember if you had fucked her?" Nigel asked. The tone in his voice disturbed Gareth. He sounded angry, even though he was trying to contain his emotion.

"My client has already told you that he doesn't remember any such occurrence taking place. Can we move on?" Giles said as he intervened on Gareth's behalf.

"I am just trying to establish the facts here. I need to know if Gareth recalls sexual intercourse taking place, and if so, then did the sexual encounter become aggressive or rough between them?" Nigel asked.

Giles shook his head and he grinned broadly at the officer.

"That's a ludicrous question. If my client doesn't recall having sex, then he certainly won't remember any specific detail about an event he can't recall, will he? Can we establish where this line of questioning is leading? My client informs me that he tried to save the young woman's life, and if you are looking to charge him with something, then I suggest you get to the point and do it quickly."

Nigel looked over towards Denise and he nodded. They were ready to disclose some important information that had been kept from Gareth so far. Denise opened up a folder and she pulled out a piece of A4 paper from inside it. She turned it around and placed it on the table in front of them all.

Denise slowly pushed the paper forwards so that Gareth and his solicitor could both see it in full.

"What you see here, is a preliminary report on the cause of death of the young woman. We have been granted permission from a senior ranking officer to detain your client for as long as we deem necessary, and given the circumstances, a full postmortem is being carried out on the victim as we speak." Denise revealed.

Giles seemed a little bemused by what he was being told as if this was out of the ordinary. He quickly spoke up.

"I object to the word 'Victim' being used here. At this point, there is no evidence of any crime being committed by my client." Giles complained.

"She's getting to that," Nigel replied angrily.

"On examination, the 'victim' had more than eighty bruises to her body. She also appears to have two broken ribs and we know about the obvious lacerations to both of her arms. There were also signs of forced sexual activity evident."

"That's fucking bullshit and you know it! I would never force myself on anyone!"

Gareth made Giles jump as he slammed both of his clenched fists down on the table.

"Did the officer touch a nerve? Is that what happened with the young woman? Did she turn you down, so you forced yourself on her?" Nigel asked, his voice was raised, and it seemed like he was determined to get under Gareth's skin and make him confess to something.

"I am advising my client not to say anything further until I have more time to speak with him alone." Giles tried to intervene, but Gareth was still livid at what he had just heard.

"You are lying bastards, I saw her naked in the bathroom, and apart from some old scars, there wasn't a fucking mark or a bruise on her!"

"Don't say anything more!" Giles warned him.

Denise was rifling around in the folder, and she had a smirk on her face as if she had just caught a wild animal in a trap and she was about to move in for the kill. She placed a selection of pictures onto the table and nudged them over so that they were in front of Gareth.

"As you can see from the pictures here, what you have told us is untrue. There are bruises all over her body, but I want you to look closely at the picture of the fresh bruises on her neck. It was clear that someone had their hands around her throat this morning. Therefore we asked about the sex, why we asked if it was rough and if Gareth had taken things a little too far in the heat of the moment. It's better for all concerned if you tell us the truth now."

"I told you the fucking truth, it wasn't me!" Gareth protested.

"You told us that there was no one else in your flat!" Nigel said as he leaned forwards and he too struck the table hard with his open palms.

"There wasn't!" Gareth replied. His head was spinning badly and he wanted to throw up.

"Don't say anything else!" Giles warned him again. Gareth wasn't listening to him though.

"Then it must have been you who held her under the water, beat her up and then drowned her?"

"No one held her under the water, she killed herself by cutting her wrists!"

"Then why is it that the only set of fingerprints on the piece of glass, is yours?" Denise asked him.

"I already told you, it was because I was drinking from it and I dropped the bloody glass!"

Gareth's face had turned a dark shade of red again. He couldn't answer any of the questions without making himself look guilty for something that he had not been responsible for.

"I must insist that we terminate this interview until I have had time to speak further with my client!" Giles demanded. Denise looked him straight in the eye.

"Your client is going to be remanded in custody pending the full post mortem report." Giles knew that she was confident that she had enough evidence to make this stick with the CPS, and now he too had doubts in his mind about his client's innocence. He needed time to take stock of this whole case.

"Interview suspended at fifteen twenty-four," Denise said, then she pressed the stop button on the tape recorder.

Denise was still smiling, as she and Nigel left the room. Giles waited until they had walked down the corridor out of earshot and then he turned to face Gareth.

"This doesn't look good at all, and I need you to be completely honest with me here, timing is crucial if we are to strike a deal. Tell me the truth, did you abuse and kill the woman?"

"No. I fucking didn't!" Gareth protested. His hopes of leaving the police station were fading away fast. He felt hopeless as he saw the look on Giles's face. It was clear that no one believed his innocence, not even his solicitor.

All of you

The telephone rang once before the call was diverted through to the mobile voicemail service. It was the fifth time this had happened today, and it was frustrating. Natalie had tried to call Gareth at least twenty times over the last few days, but his mobile phone appeared to be switched off. Unusually, he had been absent from social media too. He hadn't read her texts, and no one was answering the home phone either. She had asked a friend to visit the flat, but Gareth had not answered the intercom system.

Natalie was in two minds as to what to do next. She switched her phone over to its silent mode, with vibration on only and placed it back in her trouser pocket. The annual works conference was in full swing, but she had been unable to focus on any of the presentations so far today. There were had another ten days left in France before she was due to return home, and the chance to visit the company's head office had proved an invaluable experience.

Her manager Ryan had assured her that she was looking at rapid advancement within the company, and they had shared a few pleasant evening meals during their time here. Life was on the up, and she felt like she was heading somewhere in life where she could be successful and move up in the world. She couldn't help but worry about Gareth though.

Natalie walked back along the corridor and stopped suddenly

outside of the entrance to the main hall. The conference was filled with company delegates from all over the world, who were chatting away merrily over cups of coffee during a short recess. It was no good trying to concentrate on her work, her mind was thinking the worst had happened and that her husband must be in trouble back home. She couldn't help but fear the worst as she took the phone out of her pocket and opened it up. There were no new notifications on the screen.

Natalie opened the mobile phone's internet browser and began to search for a ticket on the Eurotunnel. There were some spaces available on the train later that afternoon. Natalie kept the browser open as she walked away from the hall containing all the other delegates and hurried back along the hallway, towards her hotel room. She was in two minds about what to do now.

She opened the door of her hotel room using her keycard and then placed the card in the holder on the wall which in turn activated the electricity in the room, and the lights came on. Natalie's handbag was locked away safely within her suitcase. This was something she had always done when away from home rather than using the hotel safe within the room. She unlocked the case and took out her bag, then she found her purse and took out her credit card. She was just about to book her ticket online when there was a gentle knocking sound coming from her hotel room door.

After dropping her phone and credit card on the bed, she walked over to the door and opened it. She was surprised to see Ryan standing in the hallway outside of her hotel room.

"Hi." She said. Her face became flushed slightly, and Ryan noticed her cheeks were changing colour. He smiled at her gently.

"Is everything alright? I saw you leaving the conference and you looked like you were in a hurry, so I just wanted to make sure that everything is okay?" He asked her.

"No. Not really. I just have a bad feeling that something is wrong at home. Gareth isn't answering his phone and he seems to have completely disappeared. I'm worried about him." She replied looking visibly upset. Ryan walked into the hotel room without an invitation, but Natalie needed someone to confide in.

"I wouldn't worry too much about Gareth. He's probably just having some fun after being left to his own devices. I shouldn't worry too much."

Natalie was standing by the edge of her King Size bed and Ryan placed his large hands on her arms to reassure her. There are only a few more weeks left here, I think you should give it a bit more time and we can make the best of it. Ryan's hands were starting to move around her back, and he pulled her in closer to him.

At first, Natalie allowed Ryan to put his strong arms around her and she let him hold her. She sank her head into his chest, enjoying his scent while recalling the safety of his embrace. His hands moved down her back, slowly smoothing his hands over her backside and then he began gently moving his hands around to the front of her body. It felt like Natalie's entire body was tingling, and she could have happily let him continue further, but her thoughts returned to her husband, and she pushed Ryan away.

"What's wrong?" He asked her. His tone was that of a petulant child who had just been denied access to his favourite toy.

"What happened between us should never have happened, and it never will again. I'm married and I love my husband. I can't deny that what happened between us was great and our nights together on this trip have been amazing, but this whole thing was a mistake. We need to forget that it ever happened."

"Of course. You are right. This was a huge mistake. I feel the same." Ryan replied without any hint of regret at Natalie ending the relationship between them.

Natalie felt confused inside. It was right to end this brief affair, so why did it hurt so much to hear the words that were coming out of his mouth? Was he dismissing their relationship that easily? Then she realised just how addicted she was to his strength in being able to walk away. "I will leave you in peace to do what you need to do," Ryan said as he turned around and walked towards the door.

"Wait!" Natalie shouted to him, and Ryan turned around slowly.

"I want you to go home and sort things out. I will see you back in the office." He told her and then he let himself out of the room and closed the door behind him.

A single tear fell down Natalie's cheek. It wasn't remorse that she was experiencing though, she wasn't sure why, but she had no regrets about sleeping with Ryan. Deep in her thoughts, she feared what Ryan might do with the other female delegates here, and of losing him to another woman. Then her thoughts turned back to her husband and Natalie needed to know what had happened to him. She picked the phone up from the bed and continued to book her ticket home.

A little later that afternoon, Natalie was sitting in the front of her car which was parked safely on the train heading back towards England. When they reached the other side of the channel, she had a long drive back to Andover ahead of her, so she tilted her car seat back slightly, and closed her eyes for just a few minutes. Her thoughts quickly turned to Ryan, and even in her dreams, she could not bear the thought of losing him to another.

Come Undone

After what felt like days in his cell, Gareth was laying down on the wafer-thin blue foam mattress when he heard the viewing panel in the door opening up. A police officer stared inside and seeing that the prisoner was on the other side of the cell, the officer unlocked the door and opened it up wide.

"Would you step outside of the cell please?" The officer asked him. Gareth smiled. He was more than happy to comply. He was sure that by now, they must have realised that he had done nothing wrong, and he would be allowed to go home, at last.

Surely, they had realised the grave error that they had made, and he could walk out of this station with his head held high, but not before he gave them a piece of his mind. They were going to get both barrels, and a wrongful arrest complaint would soon be forthcoming as well. The officer didn't say another word as he escorted Gareth up to the custody desk, where the desk sergeant was waiting for them.

The sergeant cleared his throat before he spoke in a deep and gravelly voice.

"Gareth Trent, I am remanding you in custody for the murder of an unknown female that occurred in your place of residence on the twelfth of October twenty-twenty-two in Hockney Green, Andover Hampshire. Would you care to enter a plea?"

"I'm not guilty of anything!" Gareth replied angrily. The sergeant then handed a clipboard over to Gareth which had a charge sheet attached to it.

"Sign this please."

"Go fuck yourself. I've done nothing wrong!" Gareth protested.

Gareth was a placid man but fearing that he may be sent to prison for something that he had not done, was causing all sorts of insane thoughts to run through his head. He was scared and he wanted to escape from this nightmare, so he turned and lashed out at the officer behind him, bowling him over and then he took his chance and ran towards the exit.

The next thing that Gareth knew, he was being bundled to the floor by two burly officers who made it abundantly clear that they weren't going to be gentle with him as they knocked the wind out of his lungs and held him face down on the cold floor while applying pressure to the back of his head.

"Calm yourself down. There's no getting out of here now lad!" One of the officers told him firmly.

"Fuck you, I didn't kill her! I want to see my solicitor!" Gareth screamed out loud.

"We will sort that out for you soon, but not until you've calmed down, then we can arrange it." The desk sergeant told him.

Gareth was breathless. He had two officers sitting on his back, applying increasing force to the back of his head. Fighting them was pointless, and slowly he started to understand, that resistance was futile. His body became limp as he gave up the fight entirely. The two officers felt that his strength had waned and they lifted him upright by holding him under each arm.

The officers had picked Gareth up from the floor as if he weighed nothing at all. The desk sergeant handed over a copy of the charge sheet, but Gareth refused to accept it, so the officers escorted him down the hallway. As they walked passed the holding cell where he had been kept up until this point, Gareth felt confused as they continued down to the end of the hall. Gareth was then shown into a smaller cell that did not have a bed inside of it.

His new cell contained a solitary bench and nothing else inside, there was not even a tap. There was graffiti etched into all of the walls, mostly saying defamatory things about the police 'pig cunts' being the largest piece of graffiti, a few phallic symbols and a vast variety of other colourful swear words. There was nothing more Gareth could do now, but wait. He was out of sight of everyone, and he had no idea what was going to happen to him next.

Hammerhead

A car horn sounded, and Natalie awoke with a start. The noise was so loud that she jumped up in her seat. It took her a few minutes to gather her bearings and she tilted the seat forward and started up the engine of the car. She had been so exhausted that she had slept for the entire train journey. They were now back on home soil in Dover.

The car behind sounded its horn impatiently again, but this time the driver held the horn down for much longer to emphasise how annoyed he was.

"Alright for Christ's sake!" She shouted staring angrily into the rearview mirror at the driver behind her. The angry man was currently gesturing towards her wildly with both of his hands. He looked livid as he waited for her to drive forwards and exit the train.

Natalie put the car in gear and drove forwards, but she drove a little slower than usual as a little bit of payback for the impatient arsehole behind. After exiting the train, she drove towards the exit and joined the filter lanes along with the rest of the traffic heading towards the motorway together.

The impatient driver soon entered the lane to Natalie's right and stared over at her shaking his head in disbelief, Natalie looked back at him and promptly extended the middle finger on her right hand in response. The impatient driver looked forward and accelerated away angrily. Natalie was still feeling a little tired, and she knew that it would be a few hours until she was back home

She decided she would need a coffee before she drove the rest of the way, and at the first service station she came across, she pulled in at the slip road and parked the car in a space as close to the door as she could find. The car park was very dimly lit, and unwelcoming.

As she opened the car door, a sudden gust of wind appeared from nowhere, and it seemed to yank the car door from her hand. The door narrowly missed the next vehicle along, and after checking that there was no damage to the adjacent car, Natalie breathed a huge sigh of relief. She stepped out of the car and locked it with the remote.

There was no one else in the car park that she could see, but she had an uneasy feeling that someone was watching her from a distance. She started walking towards the steps into the services at pace. She couldn't shake the feeling that there was someone close by, so she ran into the closest toilet cubicle and locked the door behind her.

After waiting for a good ten minutes, Natalie used the toilet and flushed the chain afterwards. She unlocked the door and peered outside, but there was no one else around. She washed her hands and stared at her reflection in the mirror. Her face looked different somehow, changed in some way. Perhaps it was the guilt she felt that in some way had made her see her reflection differently?

Yes, she was feeling tired, but now the reality of what had happened was sinking in, and with Gareth missing, Natalie was starting to regret the times that she had slept with her manager. He had made her feel alive inside, and no one (including her husband), had ever made her feel sensations quite like that before.

When she made it home, she would have to try to keep her secret hidden. Deep down, she was worried that her face might give her secret away, and Gareth might know that she had cheated on him. It was a ridiculous thought, and she shook her head to dismiss the idea. It was just paranoia. He would never know unless she confessed, and there was no way that she was going to hurt him. Natalie needed that coffee more than ever now, and when she made it home, she was sure that she would be able to keep this affair a secret, so as not to destroy their marriage.

After buying a ludicrously expensive cup of coffee and a sandwich from the shop in the services, Natalie made her way back to the car. It was raining as she walked back to where the vehicle was parked but it wasn't coming down heavy. She opened the door and sat down in the front seat of the car, and locked the door behind her. She broke open the sealed package and began to nibble on the sandwich. It tasted dry around the edges, but it didn't matter as in all honesty, it was the coffee she needed more, and she wasn't feeling that hungry.

She sipped the coffee through the small gap in the lid, but it was so hot that it burnt her lip. It took a while for her to drink the cup down to around the halfway mark, and she watched the occasional customer walking in and out of the service station in the rain. Worryingly, the rain was starting to come down heavier and Natalie hated driving in the wet, so she put the cup in the holder and started the car's engine ready to drive the final stretch towards her home.

A message alert sounded on her phone, but it was just the network provider advising her that her coverage had changed. Natalie started to feel a headache coming due to her tiredness, but she needed to get moving. It was time for her to make her way back to Andover, to find out what the hell was going on.

Falling into feeling

Inside his cell, Gareth was becoming more frustrated with every passing minute. He grew bored of having nothing to do, very quickly. The room that he now found himself in, was around a quarter the size of the holding cell, and he could barely move around. The smell of bleach hung heavy in the air. God only knew what the other prisoners had done in here.

Deciding that sleep may help to cure his headache, Gareth lay down on the bench with his feet up on the wall. He stared at the ceiling for what felt like ages and his mind wandered away. Suddenly, he heard the viewing panel on the cell door opening, and a chubby-faced male with a thick black moustache peered in through the small rectangular access flap. He peered into the cell, staring cheekily at Gareth.

"Alright, son. What they got you in for?" He asked light-heartedly. Gareth was glad of having someone to speak with and that he could tell his side of the story too.

"You wouldn't believe it if I told you. Everything is a mess. A young woman committed suicide in my flat and now they are trying to stitch me up. They are trying to say that she was murdered and that is utter bullshit." Gareth replied angrily, and then he spun around on the bench and sat upright.

"Do you want a mint?" The guard offered as he placed his arm into the gap in the door, against every rule that he had been taught. He was holding an open packet of sweets in his hand and trying to show a bit of humanity and be kind. Gareth stood up and walked over towards the door. He took one of the mints from the packet and popped it in his mouth.

The strength of the minty sweet provided a welcome taste as Gareth hadn't brushed his teeth for some time.

"Cheers," Gareth said as he thanked him with a nod, and the guard nodded his head in reply.

"What evidence do they have against you son?" The guard asked curiously. He had a good deal of experience in dealing with inmates, and he seemed like he wanted to help.

"There is no evidence. They said that she was beaten up, but I didn't do anything to her." The guard chuckled.

"Everyone tells me that they are innocent when they come in here son, but I am going to wish you all the best anyway. It looks like your solicitor has just arrived so I can let you out to see him. Stand back from the door son. Oh, can you do me a favour and hurry up and swallow that sweet. I will get in trouble if anyone sees you eating it."

The guard looked a little worried, but Gareth crunched the mint up between his teeth and swallowed it.

"Done." He said and he opened his mouth to prove that he had swallowed it.

"Thanks, mate." The guard said, and he unlocked the cell door. Gareth stepped outside. He was still in shock at the gravity of the situation that he now found himself in.

The solicitor was standing at the end of the corridor with his briefcase in his hand, patiently waiting for his client. He smiled and offered out his hand again as Gareth approached him. Gareth offered out his hand, squeezing the solicitor's delicate hand much harder than before. He was frustrated and wanted to see some positive action from his solicitor, and he wasn't convinced that Giles was the right man for the job.

He was frustrated, but Gareth knew that he was innocent of any crime, but that in itself would not guarantee his freedom. Many innocent people had been sent to prison over the years, and Gareth did not want to become a part of those statistics.

"Step into the interview room please." The guard instructed them, and both men entered the room. The guard closed the door behind them to give them some privacy.

Giles decided to sit on the edge of the top of the table rather than taking a seat in one of the chairs.

"What the hell is happening?" Gareth demanded to know. He had no idea what was about to come out of Giles's mouth, but he would soon regret asking this question.

"We have had the full coroner's report back, and I'm afraid that it's not good news Gareth. They want to throw the book at you. In essence, they accuse you of sexually assaulting the victim, murdering her and then trying to pervert the course of justice by covering up the crime. We can fight this, but it's going to be costly. It might be better for you now to accept a plea bargain of manslaughter if that is a route you decide to take?"

Gareth's face was bright red with anger and frustration. He could not believe what he was hearing.

"But I didn't touch her!" Gareth pleaded.

"The report makes very grim reading. They have some serious evidence of forced sexual activity, causing vaginal and anal tearing. There were numerous bruises all over the woman's body too. The evidence of the victim being throttled, and examination of her lungs show that she was drowned and that the cuts to her arms occurred after her death. There's also a matter of your D.N.A. being found inside of the victim, and your fingerprints on the shard of glass. Now, you need to be honest with me if I have any hope of helping you." Giles warned him.

Gareth stared straight at his solicitor. There appeared to be enough evidence to convince anyone of his guilt, and although in his heart, he knew that he was innocent, it was going to be difficult to convince anyone at all that he hadn't murdered the woman. This felt like a never-ending nightmare from which he was unable to wake up. Gareth moved closer to Giles with the index finger on his left hand raised. He started to point at Giles who was starting to feel a little uneasy about his client's proximity, but he remained calm as Gareth approached him.

"I need you to listen to me. I may have fucked her, but I don't remember. The last time I saw her, she was alive and as far as

I recall, she did not have a mark on her body. I don't understand what happened, and I can't explain her injuries, but I swear to you, I never hurt her!"

"I can call your wife for you, but I don't think that you will be going home any time soon. I need to know what your plea is going to be before we go into the courtroom."

"I'm not guilty, what do you think my plea is going to be!" Gareth shouted.

The guard heard the loud noise from inside the consultation room, and he put his face up to the window to make sure that everything was okay. Giles waved at him to reassure him that he was fine, and the guard winked at him in return.

"Are you ready to go into the courtroom now?" Giles asked.

"As ready as I will ever be. Will they take me in a van to the court?"

"There's no need for that. Here in Basingstoke, the court is adjacent to the police station. Once we go through the door, you will be facing three magistrates who will have read the case against you. They will ask you for your plea. Whatever you do, be polite to them. No matter what happens, or what you hear in there." Gareth nodded to let Giles know that he understood. Then the solicitor waved to the guard, who turned around and opened up the door.

"We are ready whenever the magistrates are," Giles said to him.

All of you

It was dark outside when Natalie finally arrived home. Gareth's car was parked in the drive, and that gave her hope that everything was going to be alright. She parked the car just behind her husband's car and opened the boot. Natalie lifted out her suitcase from inside, slammed the boot shut and locked the car. She extended the handle on the case and pulled it across the uneven ground towards her home.

The wheels on the bottom of the suitcase were unable to cope with the cracks in the pavement and it tipped erratically from side to side as she walked. As she opened the communal door to the flats, a strange scent filled her nostrils. It reminded her of a hospital. Natalie turned on the light and carried the case up both flights of stairs. She was out of breath when she reached the top floor flats.

Annoyingly, the lights automatically turned off due to a timer before she had reached the top of the stairs. After dropping the suitcase on the landing outside of the front door, Natalie paused to try and gather her breath for a few seconds. The block of six flats sounded quieter than usual. It was as if none of their neighbor's was at home, and that was very unusual.

The hallway lights needed adjusting, but none of the neighbours on the lower floors had an issue. The timer always reached the end of its cycle while they climbed the final stairwell, and at this time of night, there was no natural light coming in from the roof window. Natalie leant forward and fumbled around in the dark, trying to locate the light switch on the wall. Once she had found the plastic button, she turned the lights on and then she stopped breathing entirely. Across the door of the flat, there was a police letter affixed to the front door with blue and white police tape, that was designed to deter anyone from entering.

It was hard to breathe with the panic coming over her in increasing waves.

"Gareth, no!" She said out loud, fearing the worst for her husband. She ripped off the warning held on by the strips of tape and unlocked the door hurriedly, then without showing any hint of fear for her safety, she rushed inside.

The stench of bleach coming from inside of the flat was overpowering, so much so that it made her feel physically sick.

"Gareth, are you here? Where are you?" She shouted as she turned on the hallway light. Natalie almost jumped out of her skin when she saw the face in front of her in the hallway, then she kicked herself when she realised that it was just her reflection in the mirror on the wall. She turned to her left to head towards the living room, and she jumped in fright again.

At the end of the hallway, there hung a painted picture that had not been there when she had left. The image was something that resembled a human face screaming as it emerged from a dark void. It horrified her, but Gareth must have been proud of it, as he had taken the time to fix it to the wall, and he never rushed to do this type of job normally. She would have to nag him for days to get any little job done in the home.

The image made her feel uneasy and Natalie felt a cold shiver as she walked past the painting towards the living room, where she turned on the light. The hallway felt ice-cold, and she could see her breath hanging in the air. There was no one in the living room, so she turned around, and walked toward the bathroom at the opposite end of the hallway.

Only in dreams

It was clear to Natalie before she had even opened the door, that inside of the bathroom was where the heavy stench of bleach was coming from. She went to push the door inwards slightly and then she noticed that the lock was broken. The bathroom cabinet was open a fraction too. The bathmat was missing from the floor, along with a few towels missing from the stack.

The bath and the bath surround looked to have been immaculately cleaned, but Gareth was nowhere to be seen.

"What the fuck happened here?" She said out loud. Natalie noticed something glistening over in the sink, and as she looked inside, there was a shard of glass that had become wedged down the drain. "Where the hell are you Gareth?" She shouted, but the flat, along with the other flats in the block were all empty.

If Natalie was going to find out what had happened to her husband, she was going to have to speak to the police, it was the only way that she was going to get any answers to her questions.

Are you feeling numb?

After Giles had left the interview room, the guard showed Gareth out and led him through the door directly opposite the interview room. There was another wooden door in front of them both. This second door was locked, so the guard had to open it using his security key to allow Gareth to enter first, and he followed close behind.

As he stepped through the second door. Gareth felt like he had been transported through a void into a parallel universe as he found himself standing in the dock of a magistrate's court. There were a few members of the press seated in the viewing gallery who were busily taking handwritten notes, along with a few members of the public. His solicitor Giles was standing behind a solid wooden bench over on the other side of the courtroom. He did not acknowledge Gareth at all as he shuffled his papers in his hands, occasionally making additional notes himself.

The three magistrates were already present and seated in an elevated position over to Gareth's right-hand side. He was surprised to see that they weren't dressed in black or wearing those weird white wigs. They were all dressed smartly and looked like important business people.

Of the magistrates, one was male and the other two were females. All three of them looked to be in their mid to late fifties. An official-looking figure stood up and moved to the front of the court.

"The court is now in session, the defendant must remain standing, the rest of you please be seated." The court steward announced. Gareth remained on his feet with the guard taking his place on his left, just in case of any security breaches or attempts to escape from the prisoner.

The male magistrate read out the charges against the defendant.

"Gareth Trent, you have been accused of a serious sexual assault, the murder of an unidentified female, and attempting to pervert the course of justice." Gareth gulped down hard. He felt as if the magistrates had already decided that he was guilty, and his face turned crimson in embarrassment. "Can you tell the court your full name, address, date of birth and nationality please?" Gareth cleared his throat before replying to the questions.

"My name is Gareth Aaron Trent. My address is 25 Hockney Green in Andover, and my date of birth is the fifteenth of April nineteen ninety-three. I am British."

"How does the defendant plead to the charges against him?"

"I am not guilty of any of the charges." The magistrates were all taking down notes.

"Does the defence's legal representation have anything further to add?"

Giles stood up from behind his podium and adjusted his jacket and nervously shuffled his paperwork around in his hands.

"Your honour, my client vehemently denies any wrongdoing and insists on his complete innocence. He states that he tried to assist the deceased after she attempted to commit suicide while spending time within his place of residence. On behalf of my client, we would like to enter a plea of not guilty on all counts."

The three magistrates turned and began to whisper to each other for a few brief seconds, and then the male magistrate faced forwards to address the court again.

"Gareth Trent, due to the serious nature of these offences, it is considered that due to the risk of flight, for the safety of the general public, and not without the risk to yourself it would be impossible to release you at this present time. Therefore, you will be taken from this court and remanded in custody while you await trial at the Crown Court. The trial will begin seven days from today.

You will need to consult further with your solicitor to prepare your defence. This may include calling any character witnesses, or witnesses to the events you are charged with if any exist. Do you have anything further to say to the court?"

"Yes, I do" Giles shook his head as if to advise him not to say anything further, but Gareth was determined to have his say. I can already see by the look on your faces that you think I'm guilty, but I swear to you all that I never hurt her. I wouldn't do any of the things they have accused me of!" He protested.

The chief magistrate looked directly at Gareth. He seemed to be less than impressed with what he had heard.

"Mr Trent, I object to your statement, and I find your assumption to be offensive. The purpose of the court system is not to assume the guilt of those on trial, but to establish the guilt or innocence of anyone who finds themselves with the misfortune of appearing before us. I hope that is now clear to you. Guard, you may now take the prisoner down and place him in custody." Gareth could feel his entire world collapsing around his shoulders.

The guard nodded in obedience, then he took Gareth by the arm and opened the door out of the courtroom. Gareth walked through in a state of shock. He had thought that he might have been making his way home soon, but now he faced another seven days locked away, and things could soon become much worse for him.

The guard followed behind him closely as they walked back out into the custody area. For a few brief seconds, Gareth tried to look for an exit close by where he might be able to try and make a run for it again. He didn't fancy spending days, let alone years behind bars for something he hadn't done, and he was seriously debating trying to flee. He was sure that he could outrun the guard if he needed to, but then where would he go after he had made it outside?

He had no money with him, and no mobile phone either. The police station was next door, and if they raised an alarm, he would be caught within minutes. He decided against running and brushed the thought aside, he was just going to have to show them that he was innocent, and he was prepared to do whatever it took to convince them that he was telling the truth. No matter what the cost.

Give it all up

The main door of the Andover police station was closed when Natalie arrived. She tried using the handle, but the door appeared to be locked. On the side of the door, she spotted that there was an intercom system, so she pressed the call button and waited patiently to be answered for what felt like an age. She was losing her patience and was just about to press the button again when she heard a voice coming from the speaker.

"Hell, this is Andover police station. How can I help you?"

"I need someone to help me. My partner is missing. When I came home, I found that there was a police warning letter taped onto the front door of my flat. Can someone please let me in so that you can tell me what the hell is going on? I'm worried that something bad has happened to my husband!"

Deep down, Natalie was feeling increasingly guilty for spending so much time away, but her guilty secret about her extramarital affair was also eating away at her.

"Just hold on please, I will send someone down to assist you." The voice of the male operator said, and then the intercom went silent.

Natalie waited on the steps leading into the police station

when she felt a cold shiver running down her spine as if someone had just walked over her grave. It felt like someone was trying to tell her that something dreadful had happened, and now she feared the very worst.

'Natalie...' Someone had just whispered her name; she was sure of it.

Natalie turned around and looked in every direction, but there was no one to be seen anywhere in the area. Her skin turned icy cold as it felt like she was being watched by something malevolent, but there was still no one anywhere in sight. The wind whistled through the trees behind her, and the loud sound of an electric buzzer made her jump in fright. She felt stupid but somewhat relieved at the realisation that it was just the sound of the lock of the electric door opening, and she darted inside of the station as quickly as she could.

The police officer placed a cup of hot chocolate down on the table in front of Natalie. Once he had established the address of where she lived, he quickly realised that her partner was the man who was being charged with the murder of an unknown female. Natalie was completely unaware of the severity of what had occurred in her flat, so the officer had taken her into a private interview room next to the reception area and allowed her to take a seat.

The officer knew that it was unavoidable that he was going to tell the woman that her husband was locked up and that he would have to break the news to her about what he had been accused of as gently as he could.

"My name is officer Andrew Turner. What I have to tell you isn't going to be easy for you to take in." He began.

Fearing that she was about to hear that her husband was dead, Natalie lifted the cup to her mouth and took a sip of the hot drink. The chocolate was so hot, that it burned her lip slightly, making her wince in pain. Natalie responded before officer Turner could say anything more.

"I've been afraid to look on social media, but I need to know if my husband is dead. Just be honest with me, please if he's dead, then tell me straight. I need to know." She pleaded.

"No, I can assure you that he isn't dead. Your husband is alive and as well as can be expected, but unfortunately, I have to inform you that he is currently detained at Basingstoke police station. He is facing charges of sexual assault and for the murder of an unknown female."

It may have been easier to hear that Gareth had died, rather than being told the news she had just heard. Natalie's face dropped, and the hand she was holding the cup of chocolate in was shaking slightly. The heat started to burn her hand, but no matter how hard she tried, she could not let go of the cup. The pain was the only thing keeping her grounded during this nightmare, and nothing felt real apart from the pain in her hand. Eventually she had to concede, and she placed the cup down on the table in front of her.

"No. You are wrong. My husband is not a sexual predator, and he's not a murderer either." She stated calmly.

"The trial date is set for next week. The judge will establish if he is guilty or not, it is not something I can pass any comment on I'm afraid."

"I don't care what you or anyone else thinks. He is my husband, and I know him better than anyone. He isn't perfect, but then again, no one is." Natalie said.

"All I will say to you is that the pictures of the injuries to the woman were some of the worst that I have ever seen, and if he did murder her, then it was a cold, callous and brutal act. The woman endured sadistic torture, and she suffered enormously before she died. If he is guilty, then it will be safer for everyone with him off the streets."

"HE DIDN'T FUCKING DO IT!" Natalie shouted angrily as she slammed both of her fists down on the table so hard that some of the hot drink spilt out from the cup.

"I know what you are going through right now. We have specially trained officers who can help you through this, I.." The officer was cut off mid-sentence.

"Fuck your trained officers and your fake pity. I want to see my husband!" Natalie demanded.

Officer Turner had heard enough. He wasn't prepared to offer any further help in light of the way he had just been spoken to. He wanted the woman out of the station, but he was trying to remain calm and professional.

"I'm afraid that won't be possible. I can get a number to put you in touch with his solicitor if that is of any help?"

"It will have to do. Once he is out, then we will be suing the police for wrongful arrest, you can be assured of that."

"I will get his contact details for you." The officer said, and then he stood up from the table and left the room.

As soon as the officer closed the door, Natalie placed her head in her hands. She had never thought that anything like this would happen, not in a million years. She told herself that she was responsible, and she shouldn't have gone away. If she had stayed at home, then none of this would have happened. She was overcome with a wide range of emotions, anger, guilt and frustration in equal measure. Now it was up to her to help Gareth. She had to find out what happened that night in their flat. It was down to her to prove her husband's innocence, he had no one else to turn to.

Still Breathing

Back at home, Natalie placed the key in the lock of the communal door and climbed the stairs to her flat for the second time that evening. The block remained silent, and she wished that she could hear sounds coming from one of her neighbour's flats. There was nothing at all though. She unlocked the front door and stepped inside, closed the door and locked it securely behind her.

The flat felt unusually cold, and she felt another cold shiver running down her spine. After turning on the hallway light, Natalie walked over to the thermostat to look at the temperature settings. The heating was turned off. She imagined that Gareth had turned it off as he was always complaining about how hot she liked the temperature set, and he never felt the cold at all. She kicked off her shoes without care and left them untidily in front of the shoe rack.

After she took off her coat and hung it on one of the hooks on the wall, Natalie turned around and caught another glimpse of Gareth's new painting that he had hung up in the hallway replacing a smaller one. As she walked closer to it, she could see the painting in much more detail.

The figure looked to be suffering. It seemed to be screaming out as if the painting was mirroring the dark thoughts of a tortured soul. It felt like the creature was staring straight into her soul and the eyes of the thing in the painting appeared to follow her. The painting both horrified and intrigued her in equal measure. She ran her fingers over the oil on the canvas, and she felt the layered texture of the paint beneath her fingers.

Her attention was drawn away from the painting as aside from the fading smell of bleach, there was another strange smell coming from somewhere in the flat. It seemed to be emanating from somewhere out here in the hallway. Natalie walked through to the kitchen and opened up the cupboard underneath the sink. She took out the tin of air freshener and pulled off the plastic lid.

Before she had made it back to the hallway, the lights suddenly went out through the entire flat, plunging it into darkness.

"Oh great," Natalie said out loud. She placed the tin underneath her arm, and she took her phone out from her pocket.

The phone's facial recognition failed to work in the dark, as she had suspected it might, and she was forced to type in her passcode to unlock the screen. Once the phone was opened, she activated the torch. She walked back through to the hallway and sprayed the air all along the length of the passageway, and her nostrils were filled with a luxuriously rich vanilla scent.

She checked the fuses in the electric box, and they were all fine. As far as she knew, this was a power cut and it could last for a few minutes, or it may last for hours. It made sense for her to get a few hours of sleep, so she walked into the bathroom using the torch to light her way. Natalie propped the phone on the edge of the bath and then pulled the toilet seat down.

She pulled her jeans and knickers down and sat on the cold plastic seat. It felt so cold underneath her skin that it made her gasp out loud. As Natalie started to pee, she felt a sense of relief as she emptied her bladder. Then the torch on her phone went off.

"Oh great. Now the battery must be dead." She said out loud.

Natalie stood up and pulled up her knickers and jeans then she placed her hands along the edge of the sink knowing from memory exactly where it was. She turned the hot water tap on and washed her hands. There were no towels on the rail, so she wiped her hands dry on the legs of her jeans, and then she reached over in the darkness to where she had left her phone. It was no longer there.

Her first thought was that the phone may have fallen into the bath, so Natalie leaned forwards and ran her hand around the porcelain surface. There was a sharp pain in her finger that made her yelp out loud. Instinctively she placed her injured finger into her mouth, and she could taste her blood from a cut to the skin. It was only relatively a small wound, but it stung a lot.

The notification sound advising her of a new text message

sounded, and the screen flashed upon her. She leaned over and retrieved the phone from the bathmat. The phone still had around half its battery life, so it was a mystery as the why the torch had failed. She opened up the screen and read the content of the new text. It was just three words long, but it helped her to feel a little normal again.

'Are you okay?' It read. The text had come from Ryan. She paused briefly before typing out a short reply.

'Not really.' She was just about to send the message when she had a sudden change of heart.

After deleting the words that she had just written, she then typed out a new message to send in its place. 'I'm fine. Talk to you soon. X' Then she pressed the send button. Immediately she regretted the text when she realised that she had placed an X at the end. It was a force of habit as she placed an X on the end of all her texts to Gareth.

Natalie realised that the torch on the phone must have turned itself off for some reason, and perhaps it was a battery saving feature? She activated the torch again and then turned back towards the sink to wash her finger which was now bleeding heavily. The blood flowed into the sink along with the water, then she applied pressure to the cut until the bleeding stopped.

She used the torch to search the bath and discovered that it was just a tiny fleck of glass that had caused the damage. Natalie gently picked up the shard of glass using a piece of toilet paper and placed it in the bathroom bin. As she stood up, the glass mirrored door of the bathroom cabinet in front of her shattered outwards into a thousand pieces, showering Natalie with sharp shards of glass.

Natalie screamed out in fright and lifted her hands to her face to protect her eyes. Then at that exact moment, the lights in the flat all came back on. The bathroom cabinet door still had fragments of the shattered mirror attached. She could see multiple images of her reflection in the broken shards. Natalie looked tired and gaunt. She was exhausted, but there was no way in the world that she would be able to go to bed, not until she had cleaned up all the broken glass.

Thanks to her mother and her old ways, she was superstitious about broken mirrors, and with her husband already locked up in a police station, she feared that this might be the start of seven years of bad luck. That was something they could ill afford right now.

Mantra

As night fell, the cell lights were turned off throughout the station. Gareth lay down on the bed and he closed his eyes. The bed was topped with a thin pad, that was around an inch in thickness. It was one of the most uncomfortable mattresses that he had ever known. He was missing his home comforts already. It felt strange as he began to be thankful for everything that he took for granted on the outside of this cell.

He missed the simplest of things such as being able to walk over to the fridge and make a sandwich whenever he felt like it, or to walk down to the local for a quick beer. He still hoped that this was all a bad dream that he would soon wake up from, or at any moment his cell door would open, and the police would have to admit that they had made a huge mistake and they would have offered him a groveling apology that he would tell them to shove where the sun didn't shine, then he would sue them for thousands.

Just the thought of suing the police for wrongful arrest and then being able to pay off the mortgage and then perhaps taking a nice long holiday with Natalie made him smile, but it quickly faded as the evening went on. The sounds of other prisoners shouting and screaming in the station would keep him awake, and his hopes of getting out of here were slowly eroding with every passing moment.

Gareth turned over onto his right-hand side so that he was

facing the wall. It felt cold. This was how he slept at home. With his back to Natalie. Sometimes during the night, she would turn over and cuddle up to him, in the winter she would hold him tight so that she could steal his warmth. The last few months of their marriage had been strained as the relationship had endured a rocky patch. It felt as if she was growing distant as she became more engrossed in her work.

At first, Gareth had been a little annoyed by her constant absence from the flat during the evenings, but he soon came to enjoy having time and space to do the things he used to enjoy. Now he missed her more than ever, and he realised just how much he had taken her for granted of late. He would make it up to her when he got out of here. He would be a better man.

After tossing and turning in his uncomfortable bed, Gareth opened up his eyes and stared at the wall for what felt like hours, he was unaware of the time when sleep finally came. Then suddenly he realised that he was no longer trapped in the cell. Much to his joy, his nightmare was over, and Gareth was drinking with his friends in his local pub. Unknown to him, his mind had subconsciously taken him back to his last night of freedom, and now he realized that this was a dream, and it was taking him back to that fateful night.

He had not been able to remember how the woman had ended up in his bed, and he was determined to allow the events of the evening to play out in the hope that it may reveal some deeply hidden secrets from his subconscious. He searched his memory through this dream-state for any answers that may help him to find his freedom again when he awoke.

Gareth was out drinking with three of his friends. In his dream, the four of them were standing at the bar and chatting noisily. Charles, Paul, Shane and Gareth would meet up almost every Saturday night at the local pub. They would drink in rounds, and Paul would normally forget when it was his round and then he would disappear somewhere. Last Saturday night was no different.

The music was playing loudly, the karaoke singers sang badly, the pub was packed, and the atmosphere was good. The drinks flowed freely, and it wasn't long before someone in the group decided to buy shots for the four of them. This was where things would normally start to go downhill and gaps in Gareth's memory might occur. Tonight, everything seemed to be much clearer than usual.

The woman had not been present in the first pub that they had visited that night; Gareth was positive of that. His dream seemed to confirm his thoughts, as the gang of four slightly drunken men left the Globe pub making a hell of a noise as they sauntered down the road to the next pub which was called The Foresters. They could see through the slightly steamy windows that there was a live band playing inside, and the pub was packed as it usually was on a Saturday. It was always a squeeze to make it through to the bar in this pub, and it was Paul's turn to buy a round of drinks. Paul did his usual trick and disappeared somewhere, so Charles became fed up with waiting for a beer and he went up to the bar instead.

Gareth's memories were still clear up to this point. So far, there was still no sign of the mystery woman being anywhere

here in the second pub either. Even though Gareth was asleep, his subconscious was telling him that it was important for him to try and remember the details of the evening. With full pints of beer in hand, the men moved across the pub, over to the dance area, and the group began to sing along with the live band.

Desperate to find answers, Gareth scanned all the faces in the crowd, giving a smile or a nod to the people he knew, and to some of the females he didn't know, but he liked how they looked. As his blood alcohol levels rose, his inhibitions began to slide, and he was enjoying himself.

The woman was still nowhere to be seen within the crowd. The band played on, and the drinks flowed regularly. Gareth danced around in his inimitable style. He soon started flirting with a few different women, but these random encounters would not lead to anything further. Then he saw her. He managed to catch the briefest glimpse of the woman's face for just a fleeting moment.

She was standing outside, and she had looked in through the window. She was staring straight at him. He had not even registered her appearance at the time, but now he could see her face quite clearly as she stared in through the glass. Why did she seem to be staring through the window while looking at him specifically?

Gareth suddenly felt his body becoming much warmer. His body was sweating profusely, just as he had been during that night in the Foresters. It was always warm in the pub, no matter the time of year. He was desperate for this dream to continue, so the subdued memories might rise to the surface and reveal the truth about what had happened later that night. His sheets and pillowcase were now soaking wet with sweat, and he could feel a cold arm slipping under his head, and another arm moving around his waist.

He shivered with fright at the thought of someone coming out from his dream and into his cell. He turned around, his eyes wide open, and found himself staring into hollowed eye sockets of a pale white face. It was her, the poor murdered woman, in front of him as clear as day.

The woman's lips were blue, and she had scars all over her body where she had been cut open for the coroner to perform the post mortem examination on her body.

"I feel so cold down here, will you hold me and keep me warm?" She begged him. Then the woman rolled on top of him and her organs and intestines slowly slid out from her icy cold body, covering his entire chest. Gareth wanted to scream, and as the naked woman started to grind down on his penis, he could not hold back his fear any longer.

"No! Get away from me!" He protested, shouting at the top of his voice, begging her to stop.

His eyes opened wide, and Gareth scanned around the shadows from the bed. His breathing was heavy, and he felt terrified. He bolted upright before jumping out of the bed and he began searching all around the cell for the woman. The dream was so vivid, that he was positive that she would still be here in the cell with him. With his back pressed against the wall, he scanned every corner of the cell with his eyes, until he started to calm down.

He finally managed to calm down and reassure himself, that it was just a nightmare.

"It's not real. It was just a dream." He told himself out loud repeatedly until he calmed down his heart rate. Then the flap on the cell door opened sending a beam of light into the cell.

"Is everything alright in there? What's all the shouting about?" The guard asked him angrily. He wasn't happy about being disturbed by anyone so early in the morning.

"Nothing. I'm sorry for the noise. I was just having a bad dream." Gareth replied.

"Try counting sheep." He said unhelpfully. "Just keep it down in there." The guard warned as he closed the flap on the cell door. Gareth remained sitting down against the wall, he was too afraid to go back to sleep again, and he sat in silence until the light of day came flooding in through the window of his cell.

On broken vows

Natalie opened the cleaning cupboard in the hallway, and she took out the dustpan and brush from inside. She carefully gathered up all the pieces of the broken mirror and swept them up into the pan. She tipped the sharp shards of glass into an old box that was lying around in the conservatory and sealed the box with tape before she put it in the bin. She would have felt guilty if the dustmen cut themselves on the broken mirror.

Still needing her sleep, Natalie made her way back into the hallway where she opened the airing cupboard and she found a fitted sheet, some pillowcases and a colour-coordinated duvet cover. She was a little concerned about what she might find when she walked into the bedroom, but she badly needed to close her eyes and sleep in her bed.

It felt odd knowing that she would have to make the bed when it was dark outside, as she would normally change the bedsheets first thing on a Saturday morning. It was just part of her cleaning ritual on the weekend. As she carried the linen to the bedroom, she opened the door apprehensively and turned on the light. She peered into the room, feeling how cold it was inside.

She could smell Gareth's aftershave as she walked into the bedroom. The aftershave he wore on nights out, was called Spicebomb and it was his favourite scent, she would recognise it anywhere. He would always treat himself to a bottle whenever they went abroad together, and she had no complaints about how much it cost, as she loved the smell of it too.

Natalie didn't need to strip down the bed. The entire set of bedding was gone, and she assumed the police had taken it as evidence. She placed the snug black cotton fitted sheet over the mattress, and then covered the pillows with the fresh pillowcases. She always struggled with the duvet cover and would often need Gareth to help her with it. Tonight, was no exception. After a few minutes of trying to place the cover on properly, she suddenly burst into tears.

The frustration and stress of the last few hours had suddenly hit her, along with the thought that her husband might have fucked someone on their bed while she was away. Natalie felt a lump in her throat and gulped down hard. She was angry with him, and she felt hurt and betrayed. Natalie knew that she had no right to judge him, as she too had been guilty of an extramarital affair. Her mind raced as she thought back to how her affair with Ryan had begun.

Ryan had always been pleasant on the eye to her, and when they had started working on a project together. They found themselves working late into the night on many occasions. One night, after a particularly draining session, they realised they were alone in the building and Ryan had asked her if she would join him for a glass of wine.

This was the first time that Natalie had noticed that Ryan had a cheeky smile on his face and a sly twinkle in his eye. Working with Ryan was enjoyable, and she needed some fun. Gareth had been moody of late, and he was complaining that she was spending too much time at the office. She had tried to explain the importance of the project she was committed to completing, but Gareth was stubborn in his ways and would not listen to her.

She was becoming increasingly frustrated in the relationship and their sex life was almost non-existent. On the few occasions that they had made love recently, it was quick and unenjoyable. He made her feel unimportant, but Ryan had always paid a lot more attention to her, so she had little hesitation in agreeing to join him for a drink after work.

To cover herself, Natalie sent Gareth a text to say that she was going out with the girls from work for a few drinks, he had replied to her text with just a single word. It said 'fine'. For some reason, this annoyed her incredibly. Ryan and Natalie took a taxi from work that drove them straight to a cocktail bar in the middle of the town. Ryan ordered an expensive bottle of red wine to start with. The pair chatted away merrily and as they both relaxed, Natalie was pleased to see a different side of Ryan.

She realised that she was having some real fun for the first time in months while her miserable husband stayed at home sulking and drinking beer from the fridge. During the evening, the pair drank another two bottles of wine before becoming more adventurous and trying a selection of the exciting-sounding cocktails that were on the menu.

As the pair continued to consume more and more alcohol, the sound of laughter grew louder between them until Natalie's sides began to hurt from laughing so much. She could happily spend days listening to Ryan's funny stories, and of course, it also helped that she found him incredibly attractive as well as a fun companion. The pair left the cocktail bar around midnight and Ryan escorted Natalie to the taxi office. Ryan ordered her a taxi to take her home, and then he waited in the office with her for the car to arrive.

When the operator called out Natalie's name, the couple walked outside of the office to where the taxi was waiting for them. Ryan hugged Natalie, and his embrace felt so strong that Natalie knew there and then that she wanted him. He kissed her on the left cheek, but as he went to move across to kiss her right cheek, she took his head between her hands, and she met his lips with a deep and longing kiss.

He held his arms around her tightly and Natalie felt as if she was melting. The kiss between them was relatively fleeting, but it was enough to leave her yearning for more. Ryan seemed to be regretting letting it happen and he had been the one who had broken off the kiss. He opened the door of the taxi for her, and he waited for her to step inside. He did not say another word to Natalie, but he was smiling.

"Get in the car with me." She told him.

"But I live in the opposite direction." He protested.

"Well, I'm not ready to go home yet, so let's both go back to yours and have a few more drinks then?" She suggested.

"Are you sure?" He asked, knowing full well that she wanted something more than just alcohol from him. She gently nodded her response and smiled at him. Natalie shifted over on the back seat and Ryan climbed slowly into the rear of the car with her.

The taxi driver stared into the rear-view mirror and looked at Ryan.

"Hockney Green?" He asked, just to confirm where they were heading.

"No, slight change of plan. Can you take us to Copse Lane Manor instead please?" Ryan replied.

"No problem." The driver nodded. It was just a few miles up the road, and it was an easy fare. As the taxi driver pulled away, Ryan placed his hand down on Natalie's thigh.

Natalie leaned into Ryan as he slowly moved his hand along the black stocking on her leg, watching as it disappeared beneath her skirt. She did not resist, instead, she gently placed her hand on his lap and slowly started to massage his groin at the same time. By the time the taxi had reached Ryans' house, they were both filled with desire for each other. Ryan gave the driver a twenty-pound note and told him to keep the change, and he wasn't going to argue.

As the taxi drove away up the long gravel drive, Ryan unlocked the door and the pair stepped inside of the house, and after ripping each other's clothes off, they were fucking hard on the hallway floor. At one in the morning, she was screaming out in pleasure, loud enough to wake the nearest neighbours across the field, but she continued without a single care in the world. It felt like being in love for the first time in her life as she came repeatedly.

They had both moved upstairs to one of the spare bedrooms where eventually they collapsed exhausted. Natalie had showered with Ryan and then he ordered her a taxi to take her home at four in the morning. If she had a choice, then she would have stayed the night. When he kissed her goodbye at the door, she felt her entire body tingling. The taxi dropped Natalie off on the main road close to her flat. As she carefully unlocked the door, she crept into the bedroom.

As she moved around to her side of the bed, Gareth was passed out while lying on his side and snoring loudly. She undressed and gently lay down on the bed with her back to him, she was desperate not to wake him. Natalie was not feeling any guilt at all, and that may have been the amount of alcohol that she had drunk, or because she was no longer feeling the same connection with Gareth that they had shared before. She craved something more from her boring mundane life, and the sense of danger of what just happened had excited her. The sex had been incredible too.

Suddenly Natalie's mind snapped back to reality. She was in the bedroom alone while her husband was locked away in another town. She moved over on the bed to the side of the mattress where she always slept, and she pulled the messy looking duvet over her. Despite being exhausted, she could not keep her eyes closed for long and her mind was asking too many questions.

If Gareth had fucked the woman in the couple's bed, this is where the woman would have been lying afterwards. Natalie knew Gareth might not have been able to perform and even if he had, the woman would have probably felt disappointed, especially if he had been drinking with his friends. Natalie couldn't stand any of them. It didn't matter anymore. This was her bed, and now she was reclaiming her rightful place. The light was still switched on in the bedroom, but Natalie no longer cared. She closed her eyes for just a few seconds, and she was soon asleep. When she dreamt, it was not about Ryan or Gareth, oddly enough, she dreamt of sheep.

Frozen

After spending an uneventful Sunday with his family watching television, Giles entered his office just after nine on Monday morning, and he sat down to review the case files that had been left on his desk. His assistant Maisey had been working on one of the files through the weekend, and he was astonished at how thorough her work had been. He read everything that she had typed up from his notes, and then he flicked over to the full post-mortem report. The unknown woman appeared to have suffered an inordinate number of injuries over her relatively short life.

The medical report detailed significant bruising around the woman's neck, signs of a recently healed broken bone in her left arm, various puncture wounds to both of her arms which were also detailed in the toxicology report, and two broken ribs. There was confirmation of the sexual injuries that had already been mentioned to his client. The dead woman also had a dislocated jaw, and the cause of her death was confirmed to have been strangulation rather than drowning.

The lungs of the victim had filled with the bathwater after her death, and her wrists had been cut after her death too as if it was made to look like she had killed herself. The woman was still unidentified, but she was assumed to be around eighteen years of age. If his client had murdered the woman, then he did so in a cold and barbaric manner. The odds were stacked against him, and it was going to be difficult to convince anyone that Gareth was innocent.

His client was claiming to have been suffering memory loss from the night before, but he had admitted that he had seen the woman during the morning and that he was also with her in the bathroom. Up to this point, his client had an impeccably clean record, with not so much as a parking ticket on his file. He was in a stable marriage and the couple both held respectable jobs. The client's wife had been away on business, and it appeared that while Gareth was drunk, he had engaged in casual sex with the victim, which appeared to have been very rough. There was something not ringing true about this case.

Giles called Maisey into the office via a team's message on his computer. She knocked on the door out of courtesy and then knowing that Giles was alone, she entered the office anyway before he could tell her to enter.

"Great work on those files this weekend. I want to wrack your brains over this murder case." He said. Maisey sat down in the chair on the opposite side of the desk and stared at her employer. She was curious what he was going to ask, but she too found the case confusing.

"It's rather odd, isn't it?" She stated.

"Odd is an understatement. Can you tell me what you thought when you read the case file?" Giles asked.

He liked to listen to Maisey's opinions, she had a wise head on her shoulders and an inbuilt automatic bullshit filter. She did not suffer fools gladly.

"To me, a hot-blooded male was seeking an opportunistic fuck while his wife was away. If I were in his position, then first thing in the morning, I would have been ushering that woman out of the flat before the neighbours had a chance to see her. Chances are someone would mention it to his wife, even if they said it by accident. Also, if he did kill her, then why try to stop the bleeding by wrapping the towels around her wrists, it could be an attempt at concealment, but I don't think so?" Giles concurred with pretty much everything she had said.

"Between you and I, at first glance, I saw this as a one-night stand that went badly wrong. Maybe she had found out that he was married, and she became angry, or maybe she threatened to blackmail him. The events of the morning just don't make any sense though. He allowed her to use the bathroom, not expecting her to take a bath while she was in there."

"It's those missing few hours, if we can find out what happened, then that might make all the difference. Where did he meet the woman, and how did they end up back at his flat? More importantly, why can't he remember what happened? I mean I've been drunk before, but I've always recalled what happened over the next few days, normally through a series of somewhat embarrassing flashbacks." Maisey's face became a little flushed upon making her confession. Giles laughed at her embarrassment.

"We have all been there." He admitted.

"Is the client a recreational drug user?"

"He said that he is not. He told me that he just partakes in alcohol."

"Then we better hope that some new information comes to light in the next week, or your client is probably going to go down for murder."

"I know," Giles admitted. He was feeling more uncomfortable about this case by the hour. "I'm going to have to speak with his wife this morning and let her know what has happened. Can you get me her number please?"

"It's on the last page of the case file for you. Coffee?"

Maisey stood up from the chair and adjusted her skirt. She already knew that Giles would say yes to a coffee, and she started walking over to the coffee machine.

"Please," Giles replied, his face still buried deep in the case file. He found the phone number for Natalie exactly where Maisey said it would be and picked up the phone.

Your deeper touch

After having the strangest of dreams, Natalie opened her eyes and turned over to cuddle up to Gareth, but he wasn't there. It took her a few seconds to realise why he wasn't in the bed with her. Truthfully, she had hoped that this was all just a bad dream, but with every second that passed, it felt more real. She looked over at the alarm clock. The glowing red figures on the digital display told her that it was just gone nine in the morning. She rolled over onto her back and stared up at the ceiling. She was thinking about Ryan as her hands started to move down her body. Her train of thought was broken by her mobile phone vibrating on the bedside table.

Natalie swung her legs out of the bed and took a look at the phone screen. It was a call from a number that she did not recognise. She rejected the call, thinking it was one of those annoying cold callers who pestered her with unrequested sales calls constantly. Natalie put the phone down, stood upright and stretched her arms out to the sides and yawned. Her legs ached as she walked out of the bedroom and into the hallway. The flat felt cold again, so she turned up the heating. Natalie was positive that she had turned the heating up before she went to bed, but after all that had happened during the last few days, she thought that she may have been mistaken.

She walked into the bathroom and turned the shower on to

allow the water to warm up, and then she put the seat down and sat down on the toilet. After taking a much-needed pee, she flushed the chain and washed her hands in the sink. Natalie stared at her reflection in the remaining shards of broken mirrors that were left on the bathroom cabinet door. There were dark circles under her eyes, and she knew that she needed more rest. She turned around and stepped into the shower, and let the hot water strike her face and body. It felt good to be back in her flat again, despite what had happened here.

An image of Ryan flashed into her mind, and she recalled the excitement of being able to spend the whole night with him. Slowly she let her hands follow the warm drops of water down from her erect nipples, gently caressing her skin. She closed her eyes as two fingers slipped deep inside tenderly exploring every place that Ryan had touched. Then she felt a tingling sensation on the back of her neck, and then something moving up and down her spine. She brushed the back of her neck, and she felt something slide against her leg, she turned around so the water could run down her back and stared in horror at the numerous spiders floating in the water by her feet.

Natalie yelped and jumped out of the shower as quickly as she could, screaming as a spider crawled over the left cheek of her face. She brushed it into the bath with the back of her hand, she hated spiders with a passion. She grabbed a towel and rubbed her hair, shoulders and back to make sure that there were no more of the creatures on her body, then she grabbed the shower and aimed it at the spiders in the bottom of the bath who were trying unsuccessfully to escape by climbing up the slippery sides of the bath.

She watched as the spider's legs contracted and one by one the creatures went down the plughole. It was cruel, but she couldn't help herself. After picking up a fresh towel from the pile, Natalie walked hurriedly out of the bathroom and into her bedroom where she dried herself off and then started to get dressed. She jumped nervously as her phone vibrated again. As she picked the phone up, she could see that it was the same number from earlier, and whoever this was, they had tried to call her three times. This time they had left a voicemail message, so she called the voicemail number and then activated the speaker of the phone.

The message on the phone was from a male. He sounded very upper class, highly educated and well-spoken.

"Good morning. My name is Giles Morton, of Morton and Baxter solicitors. I am acting on behalf of your husband Gareth and I will be representing him at trial. I was wondering if we could arrange a meeting to discuss your husband's case in further detail and I would appreciate it if you could call me back on this number. I look forward to speaking with you." Then the caller hung up.

Natalie continued to dress, throwing on her bra and a t-shirt and then she walked out of the bedroom and through to the kitchen. She placed fresh water in the kettle and turned the power on. When the kettle had boiled, she made herself a strong cup of coffee and she took the mug and her phone out into the art studio and sat down on a chair. She took a few sips of the coffee, knowing it help revive her, and then she picked up her phone and called back the solicitor. Giles answered the call on the third ring.

"Giles Morton, Morton and Baxter." He said brashly.

"This is Natalie Chambers. You called me earlier and left a message about my husband Gareth."

"Ah yes. Good morning, Mrs Chambers. I am so sorry that you are having to go through this situation, but we will do our best to have your husband freed as soon as we can. Do you mind if I call you Natalie?" Giles asked, wanting the conversation to feel a little more down to earth.

"No, that's fine. What can I do for you?" She wanted to know how she might be able to help.

"I was wondering if you were free to pop into my office this afternoon. I have a free slot around one o clock, just before I have a court appearance. Would that be convenient for you?"

"One is fine for me. Where is your office?" Natalie had no idea where any of the solicitors were based in Andover as she had never needed to use one before, other than when the couple had bought the flat a few years back and Gareth had been the one who had arranged it all.

"We are at eighteen Bridge Street, directly opposite the Bridge Cafe. Do you know where that is?" Without meaning to, Giles's tone came across as condescending.

"Yes, I think so. I have lived in Andover since I was seven years old." She replied.

"Err, great." Giles had realised his mistake and wanted to end the call as soon as possible to avoid any further embarrassment. "Great. We will see you at one this afternoon."

Giles was just about to put the phone down when Natalie asked him an unexpected question.

"What is this going to cost me?" She asked him. Giles knew that this was not going to be cheap, but he wasn't prepared to mention the monetary costs over the phone, partly because his rates were higher than most other local solicitors and in case she decided not to attend his office and seek other legal advice elsewhere.

"Let's try not to worry about that for now. The important thing is that we meet to go over the case against your husband in further detail, and we can discuss my fees later on." There was a slight pause before Natalie replied, and Gareth waited patiently for her to respond.

"Okay. I will come in this afternoon."

"I look forward to seeing you then," Giles confirmed. Then he put the phone down and went back to reading his case files. Natalie placed the phone down on the side and walked out into the hallway. For some strange reason, she found herself staring at the painting on the wall. She somehow drew strength from knowing that Gareth had painted it. The more she looked at it, the more detail it seemed to contain, almost as if it was changing in front of her eyes.

Beneath the skin

The thought of spending the best years of his life trapped behind bars was something that Gareth was struggling to come to terms with. Being held prisoner inside of these four walls with the nightmares of the dead woman as his company would soon become unbearable for him. There would be other inmates for him to contend with too. Gareth was hardly what you would call a fighter. He could take care of himself if he had to, but there would be far stronger prisoners who would see him as an easy picking.

His imagination may have been putting ideas in his mind about what might happen inside, but he had seen far too many prison movies over the years that played out all sorts of scenarios in his head, and his mind was racing. If he was sent to prison for murder, he was sure that he would lose everything. He knew that he would lose his job, his flat and his wife. If that happened, then he imagined that he would struggle to continue and within a few months he would probably end up taking his own life.

The food that he had been given while in custody was bearable, but it was hardly nutritious. Gareth knew that he was on his own, and he would have to start taking care of himself and build his strength up as much as he could. He dropped down to the floor and tried executing some sit-ups but upon reaching the count of twelve, he realised just how badly out of shape he was.

He lay on his back on the cold cell floor panting heavily. One too many takeaway meals had added up over the years, and his body had grown weak through a lack of regular exercise. He rolled over onto his front and placed his hands in front of his shoulders. He managed eight press-ups before he collapsed down to the floor in a heap. It was pathetic, but it was a start at least.

He wasn't prepared to give up quite so easily, so Gareth stood up and leaned forward with his hands spread apart against the cell wall. Standing press-ups proved to be much easier to do. When he grew bored of that exercise, he moved on to star jumps and then he attempted a few squats. It wasn't long before he had worked up quite a sweat. When his dinner arrived, it was a frozen microwave meal that was disappointing.

He ate his meal anyway, despite there being little nutritional value in the food, knowing that he needed to keep his strength up. After dinner, he waited for the food to go down then he went back to exercising. By the time it was lights out, he was ready for bed, and no longer cared how uncomfortable it was as he had tired himself out with all of the additional activity.

Without the usual bunch of electrical appliances that Gareth and his wife had in the bedroom, he fell asleep faster than he usually would at home. His sleep was deep, and his subconscious mind was drifting back in time again. He needed answers badly, and he hoped that his dreams would reveal more of his subdued memories of the night when everything went so badly wrong. It wasn't long before his subconscious took him back to where he needed to be.

In his dream, the four men had danced around and sang loudly. They were having fun. Now they were leaving the Foresters pub when they met a group of friends who were walking the other way. They were laughing and joking with each other as they exchanged pleasantries and then the four of them continued walking up the road to the next pub called The Rock House.

Three women were walking with them, but none was the woman that Gareth hoped to see. She was nowhere in sight. The doorman at the Rock House had waved them in, as the four of them were regulars and they never caused any trouble. They also spent a fair amount of money behind the bar (except for Paul, who was still denying it was his round), so they were always warmly welcomed. The three women had followed them into the pub and had stopped at the bottom bar. The four men walked up to the top bar where the music was louder, and there was a pool table that they could play on.

Shane had argued with Paul about whose round it was, but Paul was adamant that it wasn't his turn. Shane was bored of arguing, so he bought a round for the four of them, and Paul had walked back down to the bottom bar to continue talking to the three women. He was carrying a full pint of lager in his hand.

The remaining three men then headed over towards the corner where the pool table was situated and joined the waiting queue of patrons who wanted to play a game. Pints were flowing, and then spirits and mixers and numerous shots were consumed until around three in the morning. Gareth knew that he had reached his limit. If he drank any more alcohol he would probably throw up and suffer for days.

He told the other guys that he was going to the toilet, and after taking a quick piss, Gareth walked past Paul who was still flirting with the women in the bottom bar, and he headed straight for the door. After stumbling down the steps out of the pub, Gareth decided that he needed some food to soak up the alcohol. There was a kebab shop just a few steps away from the pub, so he walked into the shop to order a burger. There were very few people in the shop. A drunken girl was swaying up at the counter. She was flirting while attempting to barter for some free food and promising to pay for it the following week. The man behind the counter was refusing. He looked like he had been stung by the girl in the past.

After reaching into his pocket, Gareth pulled out some loose change and handed the girl what amounted to close to five pounds.

"Treat yourself." He had told her. The girl threw her arms around his neck holding close to him.

"Aww thanks, babe!" She told him excitedly. Gareth gave her a drunken grin, and then he ordered himself a bacon burger. The girl was still holding on to his neck tightly.

Gareth snuck his head out from under the girl's arms and she turned towards the counter and ordered a chicken wrap with mayonnaise. A few minutes later, Gareth was handed his burger and he waved goodbye to the girl who was still eagerly awaiting her food. She was swaying badly and looked like she was struggling to stand up. Then she began to hiccup loudly, which she found hilariously funny when she couldn't stop.

As Gareth stepped out into the early morning air, the sun was starting to rise in the distance, but it was still fairly dark outside. Drunk people were walking up and down the road outside of the local nightclub. People were screaming, shouting and laughing through the early hours of the morning. An ever-growing number of homeless people camped in a few of the shop doorways.

Some were suffering abuse from drunken revellers. One unfortunate girl being carried along under her arms by two other girls was wailing and screaming obscenities about a boy who had abused her trust. She told the girls he had only used her for sex. It was nothing unusual for a Sunday morning in Andover town centre.

As Gareth turned to the left to walk towards the main road, he saw the woman again. She was arguing with another figure in the distance. He had not noticed them at the time, but now he was remembering tiny important details. The figure she was arguing with was around a foot taller than her. The figure was wearing what appeared to be a plain black hooded top. Gareth was focused on finishing his burger before he dropped it, and the woman in the distance looked towards him and seemed to notice him, then the pair became silent as they moved away in a hurry.

Even though Gareth was now walking in the same direction as the couple towards his home, there was no sign of them as he reached the main road. He was starting the fifteen-minute walk back to his flat, and he hoped that it may help to sober him up slightly. He had the place to himself, but Natalie hated it when he left the flat in a mess, and tomorrow he promised himself that he would start to clean the place up

The footpath leading up to Gareth's flat was on a steep hill. After a night of heavy drinking, the hill seemed to take an age to conquer. Eventually, he made the summit of the hill, and his flat was just around the corner. The same couple he had seen earlier was standing in front of his block of flats. They were still engaged in their previous argument. The tall male figure pushed the woman backwards and she fell on the grassy patch by the front door.

"Oy!" Gareth shouted, and then the man turned and bolted away from the area. He thought about giving chase, but in his drunken state, there was little point in even trying to catch him.

He walked over to the woman sitting on the floor, who looked a little stunned and frightened by what had just happened.

"Are you alright?" Gareth asked her, and the woman nodded. He offered out his hand and helped her up from the floor. "Who was that?" He asked her.

"It's just a jealous ex of mine. He won't accept that I don't want to be with him anymore, and he has been following me around all night. Thank you for scaring him off. I'm worried he will come back though, and he has a fierce temper on him. I don't know what I'm going to do if he comes back for me."

"Come inside my flat. I promise that you will be safe in there, and we can book you a taxi home." Gareth offered.

The woman seemed a little dubious at first, and she kept looking in the direction of where the male had run away.

"Only if you are sure?" She replied hesitantly.

"Of course, I am. I don't want you to have to put up with his abuse."

"Thank you. I guess that there still are some decent men out there."

After fumbling with the keys for a few seconds, Gareth unlocked the door to the communal hallway and pushed the door open. He held it wide, allowing the woman to walk inside before him. He followed her in, then closed the door making sure it was locked behind him. Gareth turned on the hallway light and then showed her the way up to his flat. He unlocked the front door of his flat as quietly as he could, and he showed the woman inside.

The woman looked a little uncomfortable at the thought of going into the flat at first, but she walked in, and he closed the door behind them both and locked it for safety. Just in case the woman's ex decided to make another appearance and he somehow managed to find a way in through the communal door.

"Would you like a cup of coffee?" He offered.

"Yes please." She replied and then she sat down with her legs up on the leather sofa as if she was making herself comfortable in her own home.

As Gareth walked into the kitchen, he found the floor soaking wet and realised there must be a serious leak somewhere in the flat. Now he started to panic. He lived in a top floor flat, and the leaking water would be damaging the flats underneath. He had to find the leak fast, try to stop the water from escaping and then clean up the water on the floor. He dashed out into the living room, but the woman had gone and the carpet in here was soaking wet too. The water had to be coming from the bathroom, so he rushed along the hallway, wading through an ever-deepening pool of water.

The bathroom door was locked, but the water was still rising rapidly, and it was clear that it was indeed coming from inside the bathroom. Now there was blood in the water, and Gareth was afraid that the woman had hurt herself all over again.

He shoulder barged the door, almost taking it off its hinges as he fell into the bathroom, and he fell into a torrent of blood infused water that streamed out into the hallway. The force of the water was so powerful that it took the front door off its hinges and flooded down the communal stairs. Gareth gasped for air and then jumped to his feet using the bathroom sink to pull himself upright. Now the water had disappeared, but so too had the woman.

After checking behind the shower curtain, Gareth shook his head in disbelief. This dream felt so real, and yet this part of the dream was very different to what had happened. He turned to walk out of the bathroom, and as he closed the door behind him and turned around, he walked straight into the walking corpse of the woman, and he screamed out in fear. Her skin was a pale blue colour, and her naked body was dripping wet. The scars on both of her arms had been stitched up, and her eyes were closed.

Using both of her cold hands she grabbed Gareth by the head and pulled his ear close to her mouth, then she whispered to him.

"The portal is open for a short time, and only you can save her now." Then she pointed to a dark painting that was hung up on the hallway wall.

Gareth was shaking with fright, and he almost screamed as the woman collapsed to the floor and the liquid form she had become, began to melt through the holes in the laminate floor in front of him. Her skin and bones had disintegrated, and it was as if her body consisted of nothing more than fluids.

The heart of me

Ingrid sat bolt upright in her bed. Something told her that her granddaughter Louhi was dead, and now she was sure of it. Her bed was soaked through with sweat despite the bedroom feeling icy cold. At times like these, she wished that her husband was still alive so she could turn to him for comfort, but he had passed away many years ago, and she would have to grieve alone.

Her dream had been so vivid that she had felt as if she had been walking through a flat, she had never visited before in her life. Ingrid walked into a hallway where a dark painting was hung on the wall. It felt as if an evil presence had been captured within the painting, and she touched the oil and it cut deep into her fingers like sharp thorns from a rose bush had just pierced her skin.

Ingrid placed her fingers into her mouth, just as a child does when they feel a tiny cut to try and stop the bleeding, and instead of tasting coppery, her blood tasted tainted. She walked along the hallway into an ever-deepening pool of water, towards a bright light at the end of the corridor.

The light was coming from the bathroom, and as she walked in through the open door, she could see her granddaughter's body under the water laying motionless in a bathtub, and blood was flowing from deep wounds to both of her wrists. Ingrid went to lift Louhi from the water, but the water was frozen even though it appeared to still be flowing. She stared down at the frozen body, and Louhi's eyes suddenly opened wide, and she began screaming from under the ice. This was the point where she had woken up in fright.

The dream had felt so real, and now Ingrid looked at her fingers and they were blue from the cold. She tried rubbing them together, but they would not become any warmer no matter what she tried. The cold started to move into her hands, then her wrists and gradually along her arms. Her blood was freezing in her veins and there was nothing that she could do to stop it.

Ingrid was the last of her bloodline that had fought a secret battle for thousands of years. She was the descendant of Loviatar, the most powerful of all the Finnish witches. The secrets of her bloodline would now die with her, and most of the spells that she had been taught by her elders to use in battle against the Finnish shamans, had faded away with age. With her dying breath, she uttered the only spell that she could use to seek revenge for her granddaughter's killer.

"Louhi, I command you to arise once more, to claim the soul from the one who took your life, a borer from a rock, a stump from slippery ice. Return from your eternal doom and drag him down to face hell's fire."

As she muttered those final words, she felt a tightness in her chest as the blood in her heart began to freeze and the chambers within could no longer circulate the blood around her body. Ingrid died with her eyes open wide. Her decaying corpse would not be found for many months, by that time she would no longer be recognisable to anyone.

Over my head

After a few minutes of hunting around aimlessly, Natalie found the solicitor's office door, which was situated in a recess between two retail units. She pressed the button on the door's intercom system and waited patiently for someone to answer.

"Morton and Baxter. How can I help?" A crackly female voice echoed loudly across Bridge Street through the weathered speaker system.

"Yes, I have an appointment with Giles Morton at one."

"Could I take your name please?" The female asked.

"It's Natalie Chambers. He called me earlier today, but I think that I am a little early." The buzzer on the door sounded, and she pushed the door open, walking inside.

The hallway and the reception of the offices were decorated with expensive-looking wallpaper. The first thought that ran through Natalie's head, was confirmation that this was going to be costly. She had no idea how much solicitors charged per hour, but it had cost a fortune in fees when the pair of them had bought the flat together.

Natalie thought that she was prepared for the worst, but she was hopeful that Gareth would be able to get legal aid. She could see two offices in front of her and the reception desk over to her right. An attractive woman was sitting behind the desk who gave Natalie a welcoming smile as she approached.

"You can go straight into the office; Giles is ready for you." The legal assistant said, and she pointed over to the door on the left-hand side.

"Thank you," Natalie said as she walked over to the office door.

The name of the solicitor was etched onto a highly polished brass plaque. Natalie knocked on the office door and then she waited until she was called inside. As the solicitor shouted for her to enter, it felt as if she was about to attend a job interview, and she took a deep breath to calm her nerves before she turned the handle and entered the office.

On seeing Natalie's face as she came walking in through the door, the solicitor stood up from behind his desk and eagerly walked around to greet his client's wife. Natalie looked to be considerably younger than Gareth, despite there only being six years difference between them. Giles was smiling broadly. He held out his hand and he offered it out to Natalie who seemed a little taken aback by the gesture, but she shook his hand in response anyway.

The skin on his hand felt smooth and soft as if he had never done a day of manual work in his life. His face was clean-shaven, he smelt of expensive aftershave and his suit was crisp and clean. It fitted his body perfectly, and embarrassingly, Natalie felt her face flushing slightly as she made eye contact with him.

Giles held on to her hand for a few moments longer than necessary, and it was clear that there was an instant mutual attraction between the two of them. Finally, Giles realised how long he had been shaking her hand, and he let go of it and pointed towards a seat on the opposite desk of his desk.

"Please, do take a seat." He offered. Natalie sat down at the desk while Giles walked back around behind it and then he sat down so that he was facing Natalie. "Would you like a drink?" He offered, ready to press the intercom system and ask his assistant to make drinks for them both.

"I'm fine. I'd rather get down to the business of getting my husband free." She replied. Giles was slightly taken aback by her direct response, and he moved his finger away from the intercom.

"Yes, of course. This must have been quite a shock to you?"

The solicitor gazed across into Natalie's eyes. He was trying to read her face, and he was searching her body language for any hidden clues. Abused women would often go to great lengths to protect their abusers. There were no visible signs of a woman living in fear of her husband, but he had been wrong about such things before, so he wasn't ready to accept his judgement yet.

"Of course it did. My husband is many things. He is a lazy slob, a drinker and a cheat from what I understand, but he is still my husband and I know that he would never willingly take another person's life. I can honestly tell you that."

Giles was assured by her response.

"You must understand that a large amount of alcohol was still showing in his system. He was offered a breathalyser test at the station, and on his insistence, his blood alcohol levels were taken through a blood test. Sometimes in the heat of the moment..." Giles did not have a chance to finish his sentence.

"He might have drunk a lot of alcohol that night, but that still doesn't make him a murderer."

It was clear that Natalie was not going to accept that the man she married would be capable of any such violence. In all the time that she had known Gareth, he had never even raised a hand to her, or anyone else out of anger.

"Of course." The solicitor's tone now sounded condescending, but he was just about to reveal even worse revelations to his client's wife. "I'm not sure how much has been disclosed to you by the authorities so far, but the post-mortem report has revealed that there were numerous injuries to the body of the deceased, including some of a violent sexual nature."

After initially absorbing the additional accusations, Natalie drew a breath as she composed herself.

"There is not a chance in hell that he sexually abused anyone that morning, I can guarantee it."

"How?" Giles was direct and he wanted proof.

"Because he can't perform sexually when he has been out drinking with his friends. He drinks too much, he falls asleep before he even gets started, and then he snores his head off for hours. If he can't fuck me after a night out, then there's no way that he was fucking anyone else." She was happy to disclose this information knowing that at some point, it might embarrass her husband, but at the same time, it might prove invaluable in proving that he was innocent.

The solicitor's chair creaked ever so slightly as he sat back, and he made himself a little more comfortable. This was an interesting development, but of course, Natalie could be lying and concocting a story to save her husband from a potential lifelong sentence. He decided to throw a bit of harder information into the mix to try and gauge Natalie's reaction.

"The post-mortem recorded evidence of recent anal tearing. Did Gareth have any sexual tendencies such as this that you know of?"

Now it was Natalie's turn to re-position herself in her chair and she moved closer to the desk and put her hands down flat in front of her.

"Gareth knows about six different sexual positions, four of them I taught him. He usually favours just two of those. He has never shown much of an interest in anything outside of those three positions, despite my trying to spice things up in the bedroom on numerous occasions. He tries to satisfy me and on an odd night he comes close, but most of the time I pretend to orgasm so he can roll over and go to sleep while leaving me lying in the wet patch on the bed while I finish myself in silence. Our sex life is boring, but despite that, he is still my husband, and I love him and trust him no matter what."

Now it was Giles's turn to find himself blushing. He hadn't expected to hear this admission from a seemingly rather sexually frustrated wife. All the time that she had been revealing the detail about the couple's sex life, Giles had been deep in his thoughts. He imagined her naked body, and this stunning woman being fucked while she just lay there staring at the ceiling.

Meanwhile, Natalie was feeling awful about herself. Not only had she cheated on her husband over the past few months, but she was now thinking about what Giles would be like in bed. Her lover had opened her eyes to a new world of pleasure, and now she wanted to experience even more. Gareth had been the man who had taken her virginity, and she had never known the touch of anyone else until Ryan came along.

Giles knew that he had to find his focus, so he opened the case file on his desk, and he started to flick through the pages.

"The CPS believe they have enough evidence to succeed with a murder charge. I have assessed your earnings, and I am afraid that you both earn over the threshold for legal aid. I must warn you that if you do decide to fight this case, then it could prove to be costly." He took out a letter from the file and he handed it across the desk. "These are my fees." Natalie unfolded the crisp paper and started to read.

There was a multitude of costs listed on the letter, from the costs per mile travelled, to court attendance fees, and at the end of the letter, the solicitor's hourly charge came to just under four hundred pounds an hour. Natalie pulled out a pen from her bag and signed the letter promising to pay all associated costs and handed back the letter.

"If we decide to fight the case? The charges are fine. Whatever it costs, I want him set free." She said.

"Then I will get to work," Giles told her reassuringly. In his head, he had no idea if he could win this case at all.

Asleep

The prisoner who was being held for suspected murder in detention cell number three had been banging on the door repeatedly for a few minutes. The officer on duty was in no rush to see what his issue was, and he sauntered along the hallway without a care in the world. It was just gone five in the morning, and he yawned widely before opening the panel on the door. The officer had dozed off at his desk while reading a book, and he didn't appreciate the early morning wake up call.

"Yes." He said abruptly. The prisoner inside of the cell looked agitated, and his face was flushed.

"I need to see my solicitor, right now!" Gareth demanded.

"I'm afraid that's not going to happen at this time of the morning." The officer was just about to close the panel when Gareth stopped him from closing it as he shoved his hand through the gap.

"Please. I've remembered something that could prove vital. I think there might have been someone else involved, he was outside of the flat at the time. He might have found a way to get inside. He might be the one who killed her!" He pleaded.

Things had suddenly escalated to another level, and the

officer reacted assertively.

"Remove your hand from the panel in the door now!" He demanded.

"Not until I see my solicitor!" Gareth shouted angrily. The officer pressed the emergency button on his radio to call for assistance, and then he tried to reason with the prisoner one final time.

"Remove your hand from the door and move back to the rear of the cell facing the wall!" The officer bellowed.

"What the fuck is wrong with you? I have new information; this could prove that I'm innocent!"

"You are awaiting trial for murder. You have no automatic right to see your solicitor again until the day of the trial. Now get back!" The officer was losing his patience fast.

At that moment, two supporting officers ran into the corridor. One placed his key in the lock of the door and the other officer pulled the door open as fast as he could. Gareth was taken by surprise at the speed of the door moving, and he barely managed to remove his hand before all three officers stormed into his cell. Gareth was pushed backwards, and he fell to the floor, and all three officers set about teaching him a lesson. They struck him numerous times until Gareth felt as if they were probably going to kill him, and when he felt like he could not take any more, the beating suddenly stopped.

"You better get used to that, when the other cons find you that you are inside for sexual assault and murder, they will be paying you some regular visits in your cell. Maybe they will give you a taste of your own medicine!" One of the officers said. He was snarling and spittle flew from his mouth as he shouted.

"Now, are you going to behave, or do we have to make this an hourly visit?" The duty officer asked him.

"I will behave," Gareth said quietly. He was struggling to breathe.

There was one final kick to his stomach, just to seal the deal, and then the officers all walked out of the cell and locked the door behind them. Gareth had heard stories about prisoners being beaten by the police while in custody, but he had never believed it to be true, until now. He was angry with himself for not fighting back, and their words had struck fear into his heart. He might be looking forward to years of beatings like this in prison. Tears wanted to fall from his eyes, but he would not let them come. He would not give the officers the satisfaction. He felt hopeless and afraid. Gareth just wanted this nightmare to finally be over, but it felt like it was only just beginning.

Garden party

It was just a short drive home from the solicitors, and there were an inordinate number of vans parked outside of the block as Natalie drove into the allocated parking space for the couple's flat. As she stepped out of her car and tried to lock it, members of the press swarmed around her vehicle. The press was shoving microphones into her face and camera flashes lit up the whole area as eager amateur and professional photographers tried to capture a picture of Natalie, who was trying her best to avoid the throng.

Like a knight in shining armour, Ryan came bursting through the gathered group of frenzied reporters and took her by the arm. He dragged her through the crowd towards the flats.

"Leave her alone, she has no comment to make., Ryan repeated angrily as he pulled Natalie toward the communal door. "Keys!" He urged, and Natalie fumbled through all the numerous collections of keys on the keyring until she found the correct one. Cameras still clicked all around her as Natalie became the centre of attention. She hated being in the middle of this throng, and she opened the communal door as quickly as she possibly could while Ryan covered her retreat.

Ryan managed to hold back the press as Natalie opened the door and almost fell inside, and then he followed her into the hallway and locked the door behind them both. The press were not leaving yet, they were ready to wait for as long as it took to get more information about the murder of a young woman in a small Hampshire town.

"They are nothing but bloody vultures!" Ryan said angrily.

"I know! Thank you for coming to my defence, but what the hell are you doing back so early?" She seemed confused by his sudden appearance. Ryan smiled at her warmly.

"When you left in such a hurry, I knew that you wouldn't have taken off unless something bad happened. I was worried about you, and I wanted to offer you my support with whatever it is. I must admit that I wasn't expecting to come back to the news of a death in your home. You must have been distraught when found out about the woman?" He placed his hands on her arms to reassure her.

"How did you find out about her?" Natalie asked, she looked even more puzzled.

"It's hardly a secret, it's been all over the television. It even made the national news. Let's be honest, anything like this rarely happens in sleepy Andover." He replied. Natalie's head dropped on hearing the revelation. Her parents had never really liked Gareth, and now they would preach to her that they had been correct about him all along.

"I suppose you're right." She said as she stared at the floor.

"Look, I know that we need to cool things between us and I understand that. At this moment in time, the most important thing for me is keeping you safe and supporting you in any way that I can. Do you need any financial help with the legal fees for this? I can lend you money if you need it."

Despite knowing that the legal costs of Gareth's defence might run into thousands of pounds, Natalie was too proud to accept Ryan's offer of help.

"Thank you, but I think that we have enough in the bank to cover this." She replied. Knowing full well that she may have to take out a loan from the bank or borrow funds from her family and friends to cover the costs. She did not want to be in debt to her boss. They were already far too close, and after what had happened while she had been away from home, she needed some time to think carefully about her marriage.

"Don't take this the wrong way, but with what happened in this flat, I don't think that it's sensible for you to stay here alone," Ryan told her, but Natalie's response to him seemed to be unexpected.

"I will be fine. This is my home!" Natalie snapped. Ryan held his hands up in a motion of surrender and then he turned around as if he were ready to leave.

"I'm sorry, I was only trying to help." He said as he began to walk away.

"Wait!" With his back turned, Natalie could not see the grin that had appeared on Ryans' face. "I'm sorry for snapping at you. This isn't your fault, I just don't know what to do anymore. I feel numb."

Ryan slowly turned around and walked back over to where Natalie stood. She felt numb, as she embraced him and pressed her face into his chest.

"I'm scared. I don't know what is going to happen. Do you think that he could have been capable of killing that poor girl?" She asked. Ryan placed his hand under her chin and lifted it gently so he could look into her eyes.

"It's not for me to presume anything. I know you must have felt guilty about the time we spent together but look at what he was doing behind your back. What the hell has he been up to, and how many other women has he had in your bed during the other times while you were away working?"

Her mind was now racing, and Natalie was feeling physically sick as she struggled to contain the thoughts that were running through her head. What if her husband was a murderer and a serial adulterer, could he be someone that she never really knew at all? The thought made her shudder, and she was ready to burst into tears until Ryan broke her train of thought.

"You know that I have five bedrooms in my house. I would suggest you stay with me for a few days, but only if you want to. You can have your own bedroom and you know that my house has a high wall around it, and there are security cameras everywhere. I can guarantee that you will have your privacy there, and this offer has no strings attached, promise. Please just think about it for a while." It was a kind offer, but Natalie knew that she would not be able to trust herself, and she needed to focus.

"Thank you. It's very gracious of you to offer, but this is my home and I need to stay here until all of this is over. One way or another. I need to see this through to the end."

Ryan kissed Natalie on the top of her head.

"You are brave as well as beautiful. I can see that you need some space, I will head off home now and leave you in peace. You know where I am if you need me. Just call me or text me, any time of the day or night. I will be there for you."

"You are too kind to me. I wish I could give you what you wanted, but right now, I need to be there for Gareth. I promise that I will message you later." Then she broke off the embrace and walked with Ryan out towards the door. He looked disappointed as she opened the front door to let him out, and he walked down the stairs without the usual spring in his step that she was so used to seeing whenever he was around her.

The minute that Ryan left the block of flats, he stopped and stared up at the window, hoping that Natalie would be looking out at him. Maybe she might change her mind about staying with him, and shout down, asking him to wait for her? He waited for a few moments, but she didn't even glance out of the window. He wasn't used to not getting what he wanted, and right now, Natalie was the only thing that he desired.

He had hoped that by spoiling her on the business trip that he might persuade her to leave her husband and stay with him. This episode had only messed with her head and now, infuriatingly instead of them growing closer, she was distancing herself from him. He pulled his phone out from his trouser pocket and searched the screen hoping for a text notification, but there was nothing new.

Ryan headed back towards the car park. He pushed the waiting reporters aside as they tried to question him further, and once he was free from the throng, he sprinted away. As he jumped into his car, he locked the doors and then Ryan typed out a short text. He pressed the send button and placed the phone back in his pocket. He would have to find a way to move things along if he was going to win Natalie over.

Half awake

Natalie tried to doze off, but after an hour or so, she admitted to herself that she could not sleep then the couple's bed, not right now. Not after what might have happened in the bed. It was playing on her mind, and she felt sick to the stomach. At the very least, she would need to replace the mattress, if not the whole bed. Knowing that it would only be for a night or two before she could have a new mattress delivered, she took the duvet from the bed and carried it out to the recliner chair in the conservatory.

She sat in the recliner and extended it out fully and then wrapped the duvet tightly around her. She fell asleep while looking out at the stars in the sky sparkling like magic beacons over the town. The twinkling stars in the darkness of space were calming, but she still woke up numerous times during the night.

When she opened her eyes to see that it was daylight, her body felt stiff, so she reset the recliner to an upright position. She looked at the watch on her wrist to discover that it was not even seven a.m. She needed a caffeine boost from a strong coffee if she was going to be able to function this morning. Natalie stood up from the aged leather recliner which creaked noisily as she left the seat and stretched her arms out wide while she yawned loudly. There was a slight chill in the air as she walked through to the kitchen. She emptied the old water from the kettle down the sink and then filled it up again with clean tap water.

The sugar in the storage jar on the side had a few tiny particles of coffee scattered inside. Gareth was a nightmare for doing things like that. Suddenly, a huge wave of sadness washed over her, and she felt her knees starting to buckle. What if he never came home to her again? She still loved him despite his odd little habits, and she had since the moment that they met. Now he could be locked up for the rest of his life.

Her hand was shaking slightly as she dropped a heaped spoon of coffee into the mug and stared blankly at the white tiles on the wall in front of her. Natalie jumped and quickly snapped out of her trance as the quick boil kettle screamed from its whistle at her to tell her its job was completed. She picked the kettle up from its stand and poured the boiling water into the mug.

Natalie stirred the coffee and sugar around in the mug and then turned around to open the fridge door and grab the milk. She went to pick up the plastic bottle and heard a hissing sound coming from somewhere inside the appliance which made her freeze on the spot. On the top shelf of the fridge there sat a large black rat that was staring straight at her. The rodent was stood up on its hind legs and it was hissing wildly at her. The animal was cornered, and it felt threatened. Natalie slammed the fridge door shut before the animal could launch itself at her.

She ran into the living room to retrieve her mobile phone from the charging cable, and then she stopped dead in her tracks. She could see her reflection in the living room mirror, and her skin was becoming paler with each passing second. There were three words written in the mirror, and horrifyingly, they appeared to be written chillingly in blood on the glass. The message was simple and it terrified Natalie. 'He murdered me!' it read.

Natalie grabbed her mobile phone and flat keys and headed towards the front door still in the nightclothes that she had worn the evening before. The rat in the fridge along with the message on the glass was enough to scare her into leaving the flat, and she was intending to do just that.

The road to nowhere

The door to the cell opened noisily. Gareth had been fast asleep in the cell as two officers entered, and he was in a daze as they stood next to his bed.

"Time to get up sunbeam. We are going for a little trip." One of the officers told him. Gareth rubbed his eyes in disbelief and then he sat upright. The officers were burly, and after what had happened the other night, he wasn't about to argue with them.

"Stand up and turn around. We are going to put some cuffs on you. Don't resist." The second officer told him. Gareth did just as he was asked. The officers took his arms and placed the handcuffs around his wrists. They were locked tight, but Gareth wasn't about to complain. He didn't want any trouble, but he was still unsure about where they were taking him.

As the officers opened the exit door, a transport vehicle for the prisoner was waiting and the rear door to the van was already open.

"What's going on?" Gareth asked. It was still dark outside, and he was feeling confused.

"You are on remand sunbeam. We are moving you to a more comfortable hotel." Gareth stared at the officer. His head was all over the place, and he just wanted a straight answer before he stepped into the van. The pair of officers pushed him towards the door, but Gareth managed to put his foot on the bottom of the door and push back.

The officers had encountered this little trick many times before, and Gareth felt a hard punch to his right kidney. He yelped out in pain and the officers bundled him into the back of the vehicle.

"You're going to your new home. Get used to it. You are going to be there for a very long time you sick piece of shit!" Even though he had not yet been found guilty of any crime, they were sending him to prison, and he was in fear of his life. As Gareth jumped to his feet and ran back towards the door, the officer slammed it hard in his face, knocking him backwards and leaving him with a bloody nose. The van pulled away at a fast speed, and Gareth lay on the floor wondering what on Earth he had ever done in his life to deserve this cruel act of fate.

The drive to the prison seemed to take an eternity, and Gareth assumed they must be close to his destination when the van repeatedly stopped every few seconds. Unknown to him, the van was passing through sets of security gates. Gareth wasn't sure if it was the heating in the van or just his nerves, but he was sweating heavily. When the transport finally parked up and cut the engine, it was already in the safety of Winchester prison grounds.

The lock on the door was opened and Gareth was still on the

floor of the van. He sat upright as a prison officer entered the van and helped him to his feet. He escorted Gareth out of the van and into the prison reception, where he was given a seat while the van driver filled in the paperwork for the prisoner handover. Once the paperwork was completed, the officer asked Gareth to accompany him and they walked a short distance to a holding cell, where he was placed inside. There were three other prisoners already in the cell, and it felt a little cramped.

The three other prisoners had been silent as Gareth had entered the cell, but the second that the cell door was locked, they all stared across at him. He had a wiry frame and looked like an easy target.

"What you in for?" One of the men asked. He looked quite stocky in his build, and he had tattoos all over his arms and neck. Gareth wasn't sure if he should answer, but he decided that it might be in his best interest to try and form a bond with some of the other inmates.

"Murder," Gareth told him. He was trying to sound tough, but his voice faltered at precisely the wrong moment. "I didn't do it though."

"Me neither." One of the other men said, and then he started giggling, and the other two men joined in with the laughter. The laughter became infectious, and Gareth soon became unable to help himself and he too started chuckling.

Eventually, the laughter subsided.

"First time inside?" One of the other inmates asked. He looked a little wild-eyed and his gaze was unnerving.

"Yes," Gareth told him.

"Knew it. The moment you walked in; I knew you'd never done time before." He sounded quite pleased with himself. At that moment, the cell door opened.

"File outside." The prison guard instructed them, and all four men walked out in single file. Gareth was at the back of the line.

"What happens now?" Gareth whispered to the inmate in front of him.

"Now the fun starts." The inmate replied.

"Each of you must now accompany your allocated prison officer and you will be subjected to a full-body strip search to make sure that you don't have anything hidden about your persons." The guard told the men, and Gareth's face grew pale.

"No way. I object!" Gareth said out loud.

"Noted. You can object all you want. This is a prison, and you are a prisoner. We make the rules here and you follow them. Now move!" The officer told him. It was clear that he wasn't prepared to be argued with.

Gareth was taken into a private area by his assigned prison

officer where he was asked to remove all his clothes. There was no point arguing, so he did as he was told, even though it made him blush through his embarrassment, and then he was asked to take a seat in a BOSS chair where he was checked for any electrical devices that might have been hidden in his body.

When they had finished checking, Gareth was told that he could get dressed in his prison uniform, and his items were all taken away. It was one of the most embarrassing moments of Gareth's life, but at least it was over. Now he was placed into another holding cell, but this time he was alone and left to wonder what was going to happen to him next?

Here comes the news

The gathering of reporters was still outside of the flat as Natalie ran outside. She had completely forgotten about them, and the cameras flashed away amid noisy shouts of random questions coming from the reporters. The moment that she climbed into her car; she locked the door behind her. The reporters were not going away any time soon. Natalie started the car and reversed out of her space, almost running over a photographer who was standing in the road as she fled. Her choices were limited, and although she knew it would be the wrong thing to do, she needed to see Ryan. More than that, she wanted him.

As she drove to his house, she tried to justify the decision to herself. Maybe the sex had not been as incredible as she had first thought. Perhaps it was the thrill of sleeping with a different man after so many years. She drove with tears in her eyes, and she stopped the car a few times on the journey as she tried to convince herself that she was justified in what she was about to do. She felt guilty, but at the same time she felt betrayed, and her head was spinning with all of the different thoughts swimming around in her mind. There was also the fear that Gareth would be locked up for years, and she would struggle financially. There was no way that she could afford the mortgage along with the bills with just one wage coming in, and the thought of taking in a lodger was out of the question.

As Natalie's car pulled up at the security gate, the large iron gates began to open by themselves. Her number plate had been programmed into the security recognition system, and once the gates were opened far enough apart, she carried on down the driveway and parked at the front of Ryan's house. Her boss opened the door as Natalie stepped out of the car, and she ran into his arms where she burst into tears.

Seeing that she was in obvious distress, Ryan rubbed her back with his hands to try and comfort her.

"Hey, I thought you were okay." He said.

"I... I was. But then I saw that there was a rat in my fridge, and…and there was a message written on my mirror..." It was difficult to get her words out of her mouth as she was sobbing so hard.

"A rat? How the hell did that get in your fridge? What do you mean by a message on your mirror?" He looked confused by what she was trying to tell him.

"I think it's the girl. It feels like she's telling me to leave. It's like her spirit is still trapped there in the flat somehow."

Ryan put his arms on Natalie's shoulders and held her firmly in his hands.

"Listen to me, I don't know how the rat got in the fridge, but I do know one thing, the woman is dead and she's not coming back. There is no such thing as ghosts or evil spirits, okay?" He looked down into Natalie's eyes, his gaze hypnotising her.

"Take me to bed." She said. It sounded like she needed to feel loved, and Ryan was only too happy to oblige.

He leant forward and kissed her hard, and she returned his kiss with equal desire.

"Are you sure that you want this?" He asked as they finally ended the passionate kiss.

"No. I don't know anything anymore, but before I change my mind, I want you to take me into your bedroom, and fuck me until I am exhausted and then I can fall asleep in your arms. I want to wake up next to you, and maybe this nightmare of a day might feel a little better."

Ryan took Natalie by the hand and walked into the house with her. He closed the front door and locked it behind them. Then he led her by the hand to the top of the stairs, past the bedroom that they had shared before, down to the master bedroom.

As Ryan opened the door, Natalie could see that there was an antique hand-carved four-poster bed in the centre of the room, and the bedroom smelt heavenly from scented candles burning all around the room. He slowly started to undress her, and she undressed him at the same time. When they were naked, she pushed him back on the bed and slowly started to kiss him along his inner thigh, moving up his body to his rapidly growing penis.

Twice the pain

It felt like hours before anyone came to the cell, and Gareth waited patiently, enjoying the solitude while it lasted. When the officer finally unlocked the door, he escorted Gareth along the corridor and into a small room where a member of the medical team was waiting for him. After a few basic health checks, the medical officer was satisfied that Gareth had no serious health issues that needed to be addressed urgently. Then his photograph was taken, and Gareth was issued an identity card.

He examined the card, seeing that it had basic information printed on it, such as his date of birth and his prisoner number, along with his picture.

"You must carry the identity card with you at all times." The issuing officer warned him, before issuing several basic contracts telling him what he could and could not do while in prison. The contracts also warned of the consequences of breaking those rules.

Just when he thought that he was being taken to his cell, Gareth found himself being taken to yet another room along the same corridor where he was introduced to a senior prison officer who asked him to take a seat. The questions that he asked Gareth were about his mental health, and the third question the officer asked him, made Gareth feel almost ready to break down in tears.

"Have you had any suicidal thoughts recently?" The officer had asked.

"No." Gareth had replied.

The truth was far different of course. He had considered taking his own life, and if he was locked up for life, then he thought that he probably would do it. There was no way that he was letting the officers know that though. He didn't want to be watched, or worse still locked in a secure unit where he could not harm himself. If he was going to end his life, then no one would know until afterwards.

Gareth was issued with some biscuits and orange squash, and then he was finally escorted to a cell. He was apprehensive as he was shown inside, and the escort left him. He was all alone now to face his future. As he entered the cell there was a prisoner already laying down on the lower bunk of the beds, with his hands behind his head. He stared at Gareth blankly for a few seconds, before moving around and then sitting upright.

"Shut the fucking door." He demanded. Gareth didn't want any problems, so he did as he was asked. "You been inside before boy?" The inmate asked him.

"No. My name is Gareth."

"I didn't ask you what your fucking name is." Then he giggled to himself. "Your name is bitch now. You do as your told in here and we will get along fine. This is my cell, so in here, you obey my rules. I'm letting you stay here temporarily, but this is my place. You just remember that."

"I will," Gareth said.

He was trying his best not to show any fear, but Gareth's new cellmate looked like he lifted weights regularly, and his neck was covered in tattoos.

"You should have said you were a smoker." The con said to him while shaking his head in disbelief.

"What?" Gareth was confused, at how the inmate knew that he had said that he didn't smoke.

"Fags are currency in here. You told them you don't smoke, that's why you got the biscuits and squash. You get one or the other. Shows that you are a fucking idiot." Then the con lay back down on the bed. "Keep an eye out for guards, and don't let anyone in the door, you understand me?"

Willing to do as he was asked, Gareth put his back to the door. He wasn't sure what was about to happen, but if the guy was going to try anything, he was prepared to put up a fight. The con took a small mobile phone out from underneath his mattress and dialled a number to make a call.

"Ricky, it's Jed. I'm running low man, you gotta get me some more juice. Yeah man, I got the bread. Same as last time, yeah? Sound. See her on visiting day." He terminated the call, and then he looked over at Gareth.

"How did you get the phone in here?"

"You shut your fucking mouth. There is no phone, and you don't ask me any questions. Asking questions in here will get you fucked up. You did well though. In time you can earn some privileges working for me, until then you will keep your mouth shut alright?" Gareth nodded in agreement.

The lights in the cell went out, and after placing his squash and biscuits on the side, Gareth climbed up to the top bunk. It was time to go to sleep, but it would be hours before he dared to close his eyes. When his body became exhausted, Gareth found himself drifting away, and now that he was locked safely away from the outside world, tonight's dream would turn out to be the most revealing one of all.

From a distance

Natalie opened her eyes, expecting to see Gareth, but she wasn't in her bedroom. It took her a few seconds to realise that she wasn't at home in her flat, and she remembered that she was at Ryan's house. She rolled over on the bed, and her legs felt weak. They had fucked for hours, and Ryan had been rougher with her than usual. If anything, he had been a little too rough with her, and it was a side of him that she had never seen before. In the end, she had told him to stop as it became too much for her, and it took him a little while to comply. Ryan was not in the bed, and she could hear a toilet flushing somewhere close by.

There was a joyous whistling sound, and a few seconds later Ryan came walking into the bedroom with his dressing gown tied loosely around his waist. It fell open as he approached the bed. This was the first time that she had ever seen his muscular body in daylight, and he was almost perfect in form. It was the first time she had ever seen a six-pack up close on a man, and it made her feel incredible that Ryan had showered her with affection and that he was attracted to her. He literally could have any number of women, and yet he had chosen to chase her. A twenty-something married woman.

Her mind began to race. Gareth, fuck. She had promised herself that she wouldn't cheat on him again, and here she was in Ryan's bed.

"Hey, beautiful. I thought you were going to sleep all day. Do you want me to make you some breakfast?" Ryan asked her.

"What time is it?" She asked.

"Almost twelve." He replied.

"Fuck!" She said out loud.

After jumping out of the bed naked, Natalie searched for her clothes which had been discarded on the bedroom floor the night before.

"I must get going. I need to present that project we were working on to the directors on Monday and I'm late for work!" Natalie said as she searched in vain for her clothes.

"Calm down, it's Saturday and as I am your manager, I permit you to work from home. I picked up your clothes and put them on the chair by the dressing table."

"I can't go back home, but I need to get some clothes and my laptop. The press will be outside, and the neighbours will know that I've been out all night." Natalie protested.

"You can go back to the flat in peace now. I made a few phone calls and had some very persuasive friends of mine move the reporters on for you. If you need to get some of your stuff, it will be safe for you to start bringing your clothes here. Now did you want that breakfast or not?"

Ryan was smiling at her, but Natalie was feeling uneasy. She wasn't sure about moving any of her clothes here yet.

"I am hungry, so yes. Can I use your shower please while you make me breakfast?"

"Of course, you can. You don't need to ask. What is mine is yours. The main bathroom leaks so it's out of use as the waters are off, but you can use the en-suite. It's just through that door over on the right. Do you want a full English? I can rustle you up an amazing breakfast." The thought of a fry up was making her mouth water.

"Yes please," Natalie replied, and she smiled gently, and Ryan turned to leave and make his way down to the kitchen.

The moment that Ryan had left the room, Natalie took her clothes from the chair and walked into the en-suite bathroom. She locked the door behind her and breathed a huge sigh of relief. It felt as if Ryan was already starting to pressure her into moving in with him. She caught a glimpse of her reflection in the mirror, and she felt ashamed of what she had done. She had to find a way to stop giving in to temptation, no matter how good Ryan was in bed, she was still married.

She turned on the shower and tested the temperature with her hand until it felt right and then she stepped inside. As Natalie showered, she discovered that she had bruises all over her body from the night before and it was only now she realised just how rough Ryan had been with her.

Kill me quietly

At four in the morning, the cells were much quieter than Gareth had imagined they would be. Occasionally he would hear footsteps as the prison guards checked the floors, but apart from that, it was quiet. His eyes kept slipping, and now that he felt relatively safe and confident that his new roommate wasn't going to try and climb into the bed with him, he allowed sleep to wash over him.

It wasn't long before Gareth had drifted into a deep sleep, and soon he was dreaming that he was walking towards the edge of Anton lakes, the local nature reserve which was close to his flat. Gareth and Natalie had walked around these lakes hundreds of times, holding hands as they enjoyed the peace and tranquillity of the natural beauty of the area. This time, he was alone as he walked around the lakes.

Seeing the reflection of the sun on the surface of the water, Gareth walked towards the edge of the lake, and despite the sudden gusts of wind that were blowing in his face, the surface of the water was calm and still. There was something wrong with this dream, and it took him a few seconds to realise what it was.

This was a busy nature reserve, but there were no animals to be seen anywhere. No ducks or swans were swimming in the lakes, and no birds flying in the skies above him. The water looked darker than usual, and he had no visible reflection on the surface. It was as if the lakes were dead. Suddenly, ripples started to form out in the middle of the lake. Something was rising from under the water, and whatever it was, it didn't appear to be friendly.

A dark body rose from the water. It was covered in drag weeds that were trying in vain to pull the body back down under the water, but it was far too strong for that. When the figure had fully emerged, it seemed to hover above the surface of the lake, and then it started to drift towards Gareth. He wanted to run, but Gareth's feet seemed to be set in stone, and as he looked down, he discovered that his legs were knee-deep in thick mud at the edge of the water.

He was trapped and at the mercy of whatever this creature was.

"What do you want from me?" Gareth shouted as the creature approached him and held out its hands. The figure had been badly burned from head to toe, and every inch of the skin which covered its body was charred.

"To show you the kindness you once showed me and save you from a lifetime of pain and misery."

The eyelids of the creature cracked open, and from the colour of her eyes, Gareth knew who it was. This was what remained of the woman from his flat. Louhi placed her hands across his face and touched him gently to reassure him that she meant him no harm. With her hands on his face, he could smell the burnt skin that covered her entire body.

"I don't understand. You are dead. They cremated your body, so how is it that you can keep appearing in my dreams?" Gareth asked her with confusion in his voice.

"I accidentally created a portal between realms as I tried to show you what the evil creature looks like to me. I wanted you to see how I saw him through my eyes. I painted a picture of the darkness of his soul, and I placed it in your hallway. I'm not yet strong enough to come back through the portal, as my soul was drawn down into the fiery depths of hell, but my ancestors helped me find a way to show you the truth.

I will appear and help you for as long as I can but the only way to show myself is through your dreams. I must make you see things through my eyes." Louhi told him, and it made no sense to Gareth at all. "Take me back to the water." She said before she took Gareth by the hand, and suddenly they were taken back to the morning of her death and Louhi was still locked in the bathroom of his flat.

Revelations

The scent of sausages' cooking drifted through the ground floor of the house, and they smelt delicious. They were sourced from the local butcher, and they sizzled away merrily in the air fryer. Ryan was preparing mushrooms and bacon ready to place into the frying pan, and he had placed some plum tomatoes into a pan on the hob. The hash browns were in the oven and the beans were ready to be microwaved. Ryan's phone vibrated on the kitchen side, and he walked across the kitchen and picked it up.

There was a new text message on the phone.

"How much longer?" The message read, and Ryan typed out a reply.

'Not long. It's almost done.' Then he pressed send. A few minutes later, another text appeared.

'I want more money.' It read. Ryan laughed as he looked at the text, and he shook his head as he replied.

'A few more days and I will give you another thousand. Don't get greedy.' He typed and sent the message.

'Deal.' Was the one-word reply that came back. Ryan deleted the texts, and then placed the phone back down on the side. Then he returned to cooking breakfast for his lover.

Be the water

As the powerful water jets pounded against Natalie's body, her nipples became hard and erect. The shower was expensive and impressive, but she wanted to get showered as quickly as she could, get dressed, and then make her excuses and leave the house to go back home. On the way back to the flat she would call an exterminator for the rodent and after she had cleaned the fridge out, she could get her work done.

Annoyingly, the water suddenly stopped flowing from above her head just when she had covered her hair and face with shower gel. After wiping her eyes dry with a towel, she lowered the showerhead and tapped it with her hand, hoping to clear any blockage. The water still refused to flow. She turned off the water at the tap, and then she started worrying that she might have broken the expensive equipment.

She unscrewed the top of the showerhead, ready to remove any blockage from inside, and she almost dropped the metal showerhead onto the enamelled floor. Inside the shower, she discovered that there was a hidden camera carefully concealed that was facing downwards. It was covered in a thick plastic tube that had moved slightly and it was preventing the water from flowing. Ryan had been filming her and any other women that he had invited into his house as they showered. The thought made her feel sick.

After carefully reassembling the showerhead, Natalie hurriedly dried herself off and threw on her clothes. She unlocked the door and peeked into the bedroom. The smell of the food cooking was drifting up the stairs, and she took a quick look into the hallway, and she could hear that Ryan was singing away in the kitchen downstairs. She picked up her bag and sat down on the bed while she tried to find her phone.

Just as she was about to call her friend Donna and ask her to call her with an excuse so that she could leave, she looked up along the edge of the four-poster bed and spotted yet another camera that was disguised in the knot of the wood so that it was hidden from view.

She stood up on the bed and checked to see if there were any other cameras hidden and found four in total hidden in the bed frame, and another one concealed within the light fitting. The bed was being filmed from every possible angle, and as far as she knew, Ryan had filmed them as they had fucked the night before. The thought horrified her, and then she heard Ryan walking up the stairs. Natalie jumped down on the bed and put her phone away in the bag.

Wearing just an apron, Ryan walked into the bedroom with a full plate of breakfast on a serving platter.

"Breakfast is served, my love." He said as he placed the food under her nose. Natalie's face was a little red and she could feel herself blushing. Ryan noticed her slight embarrassment, but he didn't say anything to her.

He imagined that seeing him in just an apron after his performance the night before would have made her want more of the same.

"Can we take it downstairs? I hate eating in bed." Natalie asked. Had he just called her his love? He had, and it was now becoming clearer to her that he had intentions of something more than just an affair with her.

Ryan looked a little taken aback by her request, but he seemed eager to please his guest.

"Of course, sorry how silly of me. Let's move this down to the kitchen." He replied, and then he walked down the stairs carrying the serving tray in his hand. Natalie followed closely behind him.

After pulling out a chair at the dining room table, Ryan let Natalie take a seat, and then he placed the breakfast in front of her.

"Eat before it gets cold." He told her like an adult instructing a child. Natalie smiled, and then she picked up the knife and fork and she began to eat.

"This is incredible." She said while nodding her head in approval at the food he had made. Ryan smiled wide, happy that she liked his cooking. With every minute that passed, he grew closer to her. "I have an idea. Why don't we go out to the beach for a while? We could walk along the seafront together. It might help to clear my head, and then maybe we could spend the night there?" Natalie suggested.

She wasn't sure if he would agree to her proposal, but Ryan gazed into Natalie's eyes from across the table. At first, she thought that he might suspect that something was wrong, but then the smile returned to his face.

"That seems like a good idea to me. Only the best for my lady though. Where were you thinking of?" He asked her.

"Well, I could look at Bournemouth, and see if there is anything suitable there? I just need a laptop, and I could book something."

"Can't you use your phone?" Ryan suggested.

"It's flat. Unless you have a lightning charge cable?" She knew full well that Ryan had an android as he hated iPhones.

"No. It's ok, I will boot up my laptop for you." He replied as he walked off down the hallway and into his home office.

When Ryan returned, the laptop was powered up and ready for Natalie to use. He had put his password away from her eyes, but he had no idea that she had found the camera in the shower, or what she was going to use the laptop for. He placed the laptop down next to the half-consumed plate of fried food, and Natalie pushed the plate away from her and pulled the computer closer.

"That was lovely, but I'm full. That was a man-sized portion." She said and then she giggled.

"Hey, that's sexist!" He replied, and then he too chuckled.

"Right. Hotels in Bournemouth for tonight." She said as she typed into the search engine.

A list of hotels popped up on the screen, and Natalie started scrolling through them.

"Ah, this one looks quite nice. It's Five stars, has a jacuzzi in the room and the hotel has a heated indoor swimming pool. Why don't you get showered, then we can drive back to mine and grab my bikini and some sexier clothes for tonight?" Ryan leaned over and placed a kiss on her cheek.

"My wallets over there with my phone. Take my card out and book it. This is my treat to help you forget the last few days."

"I can't believe it, but I do feel like I'm falling for you." She said, and then she stood up and threw her arms around his neck and kissed him passionately.

He seemed taken aback by what she had just said, but Ryan had no reason not to trust her and he squeezed her bottom, and then pulled her close to him. He was starting to become aroused and she could feel it through his apron. "Get upstairs and get showered." She instructed him, and then she tapped him in the groin hard enough to cause him to wince. "There's plenty of time for that later." She smiled. Ryan tapped his finger on her nose playfully and then he headed off out of the dining room.

The minute that Natalie could hear Ryan climbing up the stairs, she moved over to the opposite side of the table with the laptop. so that she could see the staircase, and then she started to search the computer for any videos that he might have stored on it.

After stepping into the shower, Ryan could not stop thinking about spending another night with Natalie. When he fell in love with someone, he would not give in until he had what he wanted. He had fallen for her hard, just the same way he had fallen for all the others before her. Maybe Natalie was different. Maybe she might last longer than the others before her. He thought about fucking her on the beach, out in the open. They might get caught; others might see them fucking. He didn't care. He turned up the heat until he could not take it any higher, and then he started to masturbate while the hot water pounded against his skin.

No matter where she looked, there did not appear to be any visible video files stored on the laptop. Natalie knew that she didn't have very long before Ryan finished in the shower, and it was a race against time. She searched high and low and opened file after file, but none of them contained any videos. Then she had a brainwave, and it seemed so simple that there was no way it would work, but she was going to try it anyway. She typed her name into the computer's search box and hit enter.

It produced a shortcut that had been somehow hidden in the main operating system files, and there would have been no way to find it unless you knew where to look. She opened the file, and she discovered there were hundreds of girls' names and dates on the files that were sorted by year. She opened the file named Natalie, and she was horrified to see hundreds of pictures and videos of her stored in there. Even more frightening, there appeared to be a hidden camera in the hallway of her flat. She tried to delete the files, but they were protected.

Then she opened a subsection that had numerous other girls' names on separate folders. She opened a few of them, and she felt sick to the stomach at how Ryan and his friends were abusing and torturing young women. They looked scared and in pain, this was not something that the girls seemed to enjoy. She thought that she recognised one of the girls in the videos, but she had no idea where from. She had to get out of there, and she was taking the laptop with her.

Pressure machine

The door hinges might need tightening after his shoulder barge to open the door, but Gareth had far more pressing issues to deal with. He turned off the taps to stop the flow of water, but he didn't even think about removing the plug from the bath. He tried to stop the bleeding, but the towels weren't helping. He dashed out of the bathroom to find his phone and called for an ambulance. They were wasting time asking a ridiculous number of questions of him. He ran back into the bathroom with the speaker of the phone activated and placed it on the side.

"Is the patient breathing?" The operator asked. At this point, Gareth tried wrapping the towels tighter around the woman's arms to try and stop the bleeding.

"No. She is completely still. Her eyes are wide open and she's not even blinking!" Gareth was starting to panic. How the hell was he going to explain all of this to his wife?"

"Stay calm, the ambulance is already on its way. We need to try and get the patient breathing. Do you know how to perform mouth to mouth?"

"No. Yes. I mean sort of…" He was frightened that the girl was already dead.

"In the centre of her chest, you should see a bone. About two finger spaces below that bone, you need to put one hand on top of the other and interlink your fingers. Then you need to compress the chest down firmly at a good steady rhythm."

Trying to listen to the operator and follow the instructions was proving harder than it should, but Gareth managed to find the spot on her chest and start the compressions.

"I'm doing it," Gareth shouted, not realising how soon this action would become tiring. Water oozed out from her lungs and down the sides of Louhi's mouth, but she showed no signs of life.

"Keep going for as long as you can. The ambulance is almost with you, but I will stay on the line with you until they arrive." The operator reassured him, but his arms were already beginning to tire. Finally, the door buzzer sounded, much to Gareth's relief.

He jumped up from the floor and ran out into the hallway to let the ambulance crew into the flat. He hoped that they could revive her, and that this nightmare would soon be over. He had no idea that his troubles were only just beginning. But when he opened the door, it wasn't the ambulance crew that stood before him. It was the pale decomposing corpse of the woman he had just left in the bath, looming in the doorway.

"You must go back." She demanded, pointing towards the bathroom where her dead body lay. "You have to see through my eyes!" Gareth was so confused that he hit his head in his hands repeatedly. He walked back into the bathroom trying to make some sense of this crazy dream. What the hell did she mean by 'see through her eyes?

He knelt and stared at the lifeless body in the water. Blood was still slowly oozing from her wounds and into the sodden towels. He leant forward slightly and looked into the woman's cold dead eyes. They were a beautiful green colour that he had never seen before, and then he noticed something reflecting in the bathwater. There was someone above them watching everything that he did.

Through the loft hatch above them, another pair of eyes peered down into the bathroom, and as Gareth slowly arched his neck backwards to look up at the loft entrance, the door gently closed. The murderer had silently watched everything from above. The dead woman had been staring up at the loft from the bath. The murderer had been there watching it all unfold. He had been there with them all along!

Killer queen

The towels felt soft on his skin as he dried himself off. Ryan felt on top of the world as he walked back into the bedroom. He pulled an overnight case out from his wardrobe and placed some clothes inside of it ready for the evening ahead. He threw in some swimming trunks, and one of his Egyptian cotton towels. Then he dressed in a pair of casual designer jeans and a shirt.

Before leaving the bedroom Ryan generously sprayed on some Spicebomb, which he knew was Natalie's favourite men's aftershave and he rubbed it into his skin. He was going to take the Audi and if the weather held up, they could put the roof down as they drove along the beachfront. Tonight, was going to be special, he just knew it.

He picked up the case and stepped out of the bedroom and out onto the landing.

"Ryan!" Natalie called out his name as he reached the top of the stairs, and he turned around surprised to hear that she was standing behind him. Before he could say another word, a heavy cast iron frying pan connected with the bottom of his chin, sending Ryan falling backwards down the staircase.

He tumbled down the stairs and landed at an awkward angle on the floor. His crumpled body remained limp. Natalie didn't know if she had killed him, and at this moment in time, she didn't care. She had remembered seeing Ryan typing in his passcode on his phone. It was a simple code that was 4646.

She opened the phone and discovered a file named Louhi, she had recognised the girl in the video, and the way that Ryan had been abusing the girl had made her feel disgusted. Now it all started to make sense. She ran to the bottom of the stairs and grabbed the laptop and jumped into her car.

As the car started up, the engine roared to life and then its wheels spun on the drive as it sped away. Ryan slowly opened his eyes and he felt pain in the side of his face. He spat out a lump from his mouth, which was a tooth from his upper jaw that was covered in blood. He sat upright, confused as to what had just happened. He held on to the bannister and pulled himself up, and then he stumbled out into the kitchen where he discovered that his laptop had been taken. Luckily, Ryan's phone was still on the kitchen side, so he opened an app and checked the video footage from the last hour.

As he searched back through the footage, he found the segment where Natalie had been taking a shower, and then she had taken apart the showerhead and stared straight into the camera. He scrolled forward on the bedroom cameras, where he could see her climbing all over the bed and discovering almost all the cameras he had hidden. Finally, he watched the hallway camera footage, where she had struck him hard in the face with the frying pan. She could have easily broken his neck.

"Fucking bitch!" He said, now she was going to have to pay for her betrayal.

I should have known

As his eyes opened wide, Gareth jumped up from his bed and clambered hurriedly down from the top bunk. He shook his cellmate by the arm to try and wake him.

"I need to make a phone call! You need to let me use your phone?" His cellmate opened his bloodshot eyes and then he turned over so that he could go back to sleep.

"Fuck off. I'm sleeping." He said angrily.

"This could be a matter of life and death!" He pleaded.

"If you don't fuck off, you won't be alive to care. Now leave me be." His cellmate warned him. It was enough to send Gareth over the edge.

Filled with rage, Gareth pulled his cellmate by the hair and dragged him out from the bunk bed. His body slammed hard against the cold concrete floor and knocked all the wind out of him. Using his other hand, Gareth punched repeatedly into his cell mate's head. Soon his face became a bloody mess, and as he cried out in pain the prison officers ran into the cell and started beating Gareth to the floor.

"My wife is in danger!" He screamed as his fellow inmate's

foot connected with his head, and everything went black.

He was no longer sleeping, he was unconscious. Louhi tried her best to pull him out of the darkness, but there was nothing more that she could think of to try and help him. There was only one thing left that she could do. For the first time, even though she would have to re-live it all, in his unconscious state, she started to show him everything that had happened that morning in his flat.

No regrets

After taking a much-needed pee to try and empty his alcohol-filled bladder, Gareth walked back into the living room, to discover that the woman had moved from the sofa. She was gone. In his drunken stupor, he stumbled into the hallway and then walked into his bedroom. The woman was now lying down in his bed.

"I'm so cold and scared." She told him. She looked desperately sad.

Gareth wanted to help the woman, but he was married and despite having drunk well over his limit, he wasn't up for a random sexual encounter.

"You can stay in the bed. I will sleep on the sofa." He offered gallantly. He was the first man that she had encountered in a long time who didn't just want to use her for sex, she had not known any kindness for as long as she could remember.

"Thank you." The woman said and she smiled at his kind gesture. "Will you just hold me for a few moments and warm me up first?" She pleaded. Gareth considered her request for a few seconds, and then he lay on the bed next to her and she placed her arm across his chest. He wrapped his right arm over her and felt a sharp scratch on his skin. He thought no more of it, and slowly he closed his eyes to rest for a few minutes.

Louhi waited until she was sure that Gareth was out cold, and she slipped out from underneath his arm. She had switched her phone off and thought perhaps this was her opportunity to escape? She felt safe here, but deep down she knew, that the longer she kept her phone turned off, the angrier her owner would be. The flat was relatively small, and Louhi helped herself to food from the fridge, she made herself a cup of hot chocolate. Then she spotted the conservatory, and she went out the rear of the flat to look around.

There was a blank canvas on the easel. Louhi had loved to paint when she was younger and seeing the assorted paints and brushes available proved to be too much of a temptation for her. As she sat down on the chair in front of the easel, she began to paint a picture of her tormentor. The man who had promised her the Earth but had made her his slave instead. She poured all her anger into the painting. She wanted to capture the darkness of his soul, and she cried as she hammered the brush onto the canvas.

Minutes quickly turned to hours, and it was almost seven in the morning by the time she had finished the painting. As Louhi stood up, she looked out of the conservatory at the view across the town, and it took her breath away. Then she looked down, and she immediately regretted doing so. Her tormentor was standing in the communal garden, staring up towards the flat windows. He placed his hand to his face as if asking her to call him, and she immediately began to shiver uncontrollably. There was no escaping him.

She took the phone from her pocket and turned it on. Within

seconds, she received numerous notifications of voicemail messages and text messages. He had been trying to contact her all night long. Now she would have to face his wrath, but it was her fault. She should have done what she had been told. She was supposed to fuck the man and then take pictures of him naked. It was a simple job. The stranger had defended her honour, he had been kind to her. She didn't want to hurt him, and she wanted nothing to do with whatever this thing was.

The phone rang in her hand, and she almost dropped it in fright. It was her tormentor, and she did not want to anger him further, so she answered the call.

"Why was your phone switched off?" He asked angrily.

"I didn't know that it was." She lied. She knew that he would know from her tone that she wasn't telling the truth.

"Let me inside the flat." He told her. Louhi took the painting with her, and she walked out into the hallway. There was a small picture hung on the wall, so she took it down and replaced it with her painting. Louhi took the spare set of keys from the key rack. She unlocked the door and then walked to the bottom of the stairs to let him in.

As her tormentor entered the communal hallway, he placed a finger to his lips to warn her that she should remain silent. Then he pointed up the stairs. He was coming into the flat with her. This had not been part of the plan. The pair of them walked up the stairs and back into the flat together, and he whispered to her in the hallway.

"Did you get the pictures that I asked for on your phone?"

"Not yet." She was worried about his reaction, and rightly so as he looked furious.

"If we don't get the pictures, I don't get paid. It's probably too late now. I'm not leaving here empty-handed. What is there of value in here?" He asked.

"Very little that I have seen. He has money in his wallet and cards." She revealed.

"Where is his wallet?"

"In his jeans on the bedroom floor." She replied.

"Show me."

The pair walked into the bedroom where Gareth was still unconscious. Louhi pointed over to where a pair of jeans were on the floor next to the bed.

The tormentor bent down to pick up the jeans, and then he felt a hard blow to the side of his head. The bitch had found a weapon and had struck him. She was trying to escape. The blow dazed him for a few seconds, but then he grabbed Louhi's hair and pulled her onto the bed. He held her face down on the pillow with one hand while he used the other to rip off her leggings and knickers.

He fumbled with a condom and then Louhi screamed into the pillow. She was in pain as the tormentor forced himself inside of her. She had known pain from her owner before, but she had never known anything to hurt like this before as he rammed himself forcefully into her again and again, and just when she thought that it might be all over, he stopped and withdrew from her, and then he entered her anally and she yelped out in pain as she felt her skin tearing. All the while, her head was held down, and she was looking at Gareth's face, just praying that he would come round and come to her aid. He was still unconscious while her abuse continued. It wasn't the first time that she felt like she would be better off dead. Then Gareth began to stir in the bed.

The Tormentor froze and then gently eased himself off Louhi. He hurriedly pulled up his black jeans and backed up towards the door. He kept his finger to his lips as Louhi turned over. She was petrified and unable to sit up. She was in incredible pain. As the bedroom door closed, she breathed a sigh of relief. Gareth awoke and crawled out of the bed. His head was pounding, and his mouth tasted terrible. He had no idea what had happened to him the night before.

After Louhi has asked to use the bathroom, Gareth had made himself scarce. Louhi had begun to run the bath and she placed her hands down on the side of the sink, careful to avoid the broken glass and she wept. She had suffered enough, and this assault was the final straw. She feared for her life, and she knew that it would take every ounce of her strength to escape from her tormentor's control. She picked her phone up from the side and unlocked it. She did not notice the loft hatch opening above her, nor did she see the tormentor lower himself down so that he was standing behind her shoulders.

She started to press the number nine repeatedly, but before she could press it for the third time, she felt a warm breath on the back of her neck, and as she looked up into the mirror on the bathroom cabinet, she started to shake with fear.

A hand clasped tightly around Louhi's neck and with one hand, the tormentor lifted her off her feet. He punched her hard in the ribs, but she was unable to scream as he choked her. The bath was filled to around halfway up and the tormentor waited until Louhi went limp before he placed her into the bath and held her down. Whilst she was held under the water, Louhi's eyes opened momentarily, and panic set in. Her lungs were filling with water, and she punched out as hard as she could, but it was hopeless.

Louhi was too weak to fight anymore, and death would come as a sweet release after all the pain she had suffered in her relatively short life. This man had promised her paradise, but he had given her to the tormentor, and he had taken her to hell instead. She closed her eyes and just slipped quietly away.

The tormentor knew that he had to make this death look more suspicious somehow. He picked up a large piece of the glass that clearly had fingerprints on it and carefully he used a towel to hold it away from the print and he drove it deep into Louhi's veins on both arms. Blood slowly oozed out of the wounds and mixed with the bathwater. He dropped the piece of glass next to the bathtub, and then he used his strength to pull himself back up into the open loft hatch. Now he would wait until the coast was clear and he would help himself to whatever he could carry. He closed the hatch behind him and waited patiently.

The ambulance had arrived with the police alongside them. What the tormentor hadn't planned for, was that the forensic experts would remain in the flat for a considerable amount of time. He dared not move around in the limited crawl space, in case someone was to hear him move. The heat up here was stifling, and soon he fell asleep from sheer exhaustion. He was awakened later by the sound of the front door opening. He pried open the hatch just a few centimetres and he watched as Natalie entered the bathroom. The woman was stunning, and he could not help himself. He had to keep watching her.

He couldn't leave the loft while the woman was in the flat. Over the next day, she had the odd visitor, but he could not hear the conversations they were having despite trying to strain his hearing. He had decided that it would be safer for him to leave under the cover of night. In the darkness, he could slip down from the loft and leave unseen. Then his phone clicked in his pocket, and he took it out to see that the client sent him a message.

The tormentor read the message in disbelief. What the client was asking him was going to be difficult, but not impossible. The financial reward they were offering would be worth the sacrifice. He started to think about how he could execute the plan, and then a rat ran across his hand. He grabbed it and held it up by its tail, the rat hissed and snarled at him, but he was not afraid. Then the woman went out of the front door and slammed it closed. It was time to get to work.

Be careful what you wish for

The gates out of the grounds were open, but they started to close as the car approached. Natalie was so desperate to get out that she drove her car straight through the gates, leaving them both twisted and useless behind her. Ryan had been lying to her this whole time. Now she had to get back to the flat where she could call the police and get some help. Every few seconds she would check the mirrors, but Ryan wasn't following her that she could see.

Natalie hoped that Ryan was still alive, or she too might be going down for murder. For the first time, she realised the fear that Gareth was living with. She didn't want to go to prison. She reached her flat in record time and didn't even bother locking the car behind her as she ran through the communal doorway. She looked back through the door glass as she heard Ryan's car come to a screeching halt on the road outside. He tried to open the door, but it was locked, and he had no key.

"Natalie, let me in. I want to explain!" He shouted, but he understood that Natalie knew far too much.

As Ryan punched the window with his fist, Natalie bounded up the stairs to her flat and fumbled with the keys, Natalie was in a state of panic as Ryan finally smashed the window cutting his hand badly, and undid the lock and let himself in. Natalie knew that Ryan was right behind her running up the stairs, she opened the door just as he bounded up the last flight of stairs and stretched out his blood-covered hand trying to grab her coat.

He fell forwards as the door opened and Natalie ran inside. She slammed the door shut and pulled the handle up as hard as she could. She locked the door with her key and placed her back against the heavy wooden door. She was desperately trying to catch her breath, she knew that this was a solid security door, so there was no way he could force entry. She was safe, for now.

Ryan pounded on the door with his fists so hard that Natalie jumped in fright.

"If you let me in, I promise you that I can explain Natalie!" Ryan shouted. He didn't give a shit if the neighbours could hear him, he wanted Natalie to fully understand that it was futile to fight him. He knew that she still wanted him, and he wanted her. Ryan was going to have her no matter what. They belonged together.

"Fuck off! I'm calling the police!" She shouted at the door. It went quiet outside for a few seconds and Natalie slowly moved her eye forward to look out of the spy hole.

Outside of the door, Ryan was pacing backwards and forwards along the hallway. He must have sensed that he was being watched as he ran at the door and tried to break it down. She screamed in fright at the force of Ryan's body smashing into the door, but it was fitted with a deadlock and there was no way that Ryan was coming in unless she unlocked the door. She ran into the living room and reached into her pocket to find her phone, but it wasn't there.

"Fuck!" She said, remembering that she had left her phone and Ryan's laptop in the passenger seat of the car. She frantically searched around the living room for something that might help, and then she spotted the laptop over on Gareth's desk. She opened the screen and pressed the power button, but the computer seemed to take forever to boot up. "Come on, come on!" She pleaded.

Outside of the front door, Ryan sent a text and now he was waiting patiently. After a few minutes, he heard the key turning in the lock. The handle was pulled down gently, and he was face to face with the man he had arranged his deal with. The man stood aside and let him into the flat and Ryan heard Natalie pleading with the computer to work as she sat at the desk.

"Come on you ancient piece of shit, work!" She shouted at the aged laptop.

Natalie had not heard the loft hatch opening, or the sound of the man dropping down from the crawl space and into the bathroom. She had not heard the front door opening either. The time for talking was over. She had her chance to be with him, and now Ryan would have to cover his tracks once and for all.

The power went off throughout the flat, killing the computer and with it, her only chance of calling for help. Natalie jumped up from her chair and ran out into the hallway to check the fuse box. She stopped at the door and tried to focus. At first, it appeared that her eyes were playing tricks on her, as there appeared to be two figures standing in the dark hallway. She knew that it was impossible, so she walked forwards, and then the two figures seemed to mirror her movements as they walked toward her, and her panic began to escalate.

Before Natalie could turn around and run back into the living room, she was pulled back by her hair and felt a hand clasp tightly around her throat. She was forced up against the hallway wall and held in place. The power came back on, and to her right, Ryan was standing next to the fuse box. She turned her eyes to her left, and she could see the hideous painting on the wall. She did not recognise the man who was holding her, but she swore that he looked something like the image of the dark foreboding figure that had been captured within the painting.

Ryan sauntered forwards shaking his head.

"All that you had to do was leave him and keep your nose out of my business. You could have had everything you wanted in life, but now you must pay the price for your betrayal." Ryan told her. Natalie was trying to kick out at the man who was holding her, but even though they were landing, her kicks had little effect on him.

"You set him up!" Natalie shouted as loud as she could, but it was difficult to make much noise with a hand around her throat.

"That's down to him. He wouldn't play ball. He was just supposed to fuck her and then I would have sent you anonymous proof that he was cheating on you. Then you would leave him for me. I am the better man. The more deserving man. He is nothing compared to me!"

"That's where you are wrong. He doesn't have to buy my affection. I loved him from the moment that I met him, and you planned this along. You are sly and cunning, and I could never trust you, let alone love you. I fucking detest you, Ryan!"

The man who was holding her moved his nose close to Natalie's left ear. She smelt delicious.

"Can I play with her for a while?" He asked his employer.

"Go ahead, be my guest. I've had my use out of her. I'm going to go and run the bath, then we will help her take a bottle of the pills from the bathroom cabinet. After she is dead, I will leave and then I will try to call her a few times, but she won't answer my calls, leaving me worried sick about her. Being the concerned boss that I am, I will heroically come here and break in the door to find that she has committed suicide. She will have taken a drug overdose and I will find her naked body lying in the bath."

Natalie watched on in horror as Ryan grinned at her, and then he walked off towards the bathroom. She was struggling with all her might, but the man holding her against the wall was far too strong for her to fight. She recognised this thing. He had helped Ryan abuse a young woman in one of the videos that she had watched.

The tormentor licked at Natalie's cheek, and then he started to unbutton her top. He slipped his free hand inside and started to squeeze Natalie's left breast. All that Natalie could do was look away in disgust while this monster groped her. She looked up at the painting. She felt as if she was about to faint as the acrylic paints started to swirl around on the canvas in front of her eyes, a dark circle was appearing in the centre of the painting.

The paints started to drip down from the canvas and pool on the laminate floor. Natalie thought that she might be hallucinating as the paint pool started to grow into a figure before her eyes and two badly burned hands began to emerge from a creature that seemed to be made entirely out of the paint. It couldn't be real, but this was happening right in front of her eyes, and she began to shake with fear as the figure became clear.

Art imitates life

It was taking all her strength to make the transition back to the land of the living. Louhi had created a portal between realms when she had painted the picture of her tormentor. Another innocent woman was about to be murdered, just as she had been slain at the hands of this monster. Without Louhi's intervention, there was no one else who could save her.

Up until this point, she had only had the power to appear before Gareth, by invading his dreams. Taking on a human form was a far more difficult task. Her soul was trapped in limbo, and she refused to pass over to the other side until justice had been served. As her face emerged from the pool of paint, the tormentor was far too occupied to notice her presence.

The bath was running fully while Ryan rummaged around in the cabinet for some suitable pills, and the noise of the running water disguised her steps toward her abuser. Louhi placed her hands over her tormentor's face.

"Guess who?" She asked. The tormentor thought Ryan was messing around with him, and he laughed but then he felt how cold the charred hands were on his face, and he released Natalie from his grip. Natalie gasped for breath as the man turned around, ready to strike out at whoever was messing around with him.

When he caught sight of who was standing in front of him, he gulped down so hard that he could have swallowed his tongue. It was the girl that his boss had coerced into leaving her family, to use for his sole pleasure. Then he'd grown bored of her and passed her on to the tormentor like so many girls before. The Tormentor had trafficked the girl out in a prostitution ring before he had tortured and murdered her. Yet impossible as it seemed, she was now standing right in front of him with her slimy grey skin covered in maggots and flies, melting in clumps to the floor.

If the tormentor had been able to scream, he would have bellowed the flat down. He could not muster a single sound from his mouth and Louhi did not hesitate as she lunged forward and pressed her thumbs deep into his eye sockets. Her thumbs went straight through the gelatinous orbs, bursting them both and the thick putrid fluid from inside slid slowly down his cheeks. She pushed down harder until her fingers dug deep into his brain.

Louhi squeezed as hard as she could until the tormentor's body went limp, and she lay him down on the hallway floor. Ryan was whistling away merrily in the bathroom, completely unaware of what was happening outside in the hallway. Natalie was shaking with fear as the creature approached her and she closed her eyes and waited for death.

"Please don't hurt me!" Natalie begged.

"I mean you no harm. I came back to claim the soul of the man who took my life. I have no quarrel with you." She turned away silently, and Natalie opened up her eyes.

She watched as Louhi began to walk toward the bathroom and suddenly Natalie reached out and grabbed her arm, stopping her from going any further.

"Don't. He's mine," Natalie told her, and then she picked up an umbrella from the hallway stand.

Tiger Tiger Burning Bright

From what seemed to be an odd choice of weapon, it proved to be very effective. As soon as Ryan opened the door of the bathroom, Natalie rammed the pointed steel end hard into his chest. She struck him perfectly in the centre of his ribs, and Ryan couldn't breathe as he felt the full force of the impact. The umbrella had not pierced the skin of his chest, but the blow was so hard that it had been powerful enough to stop his heart from beating. He looked afraid as he reached out his hands and stumbled forwards. He was trying desperately to grab hold of Natalie. His eyes were wide with fright as he gasped to try and take air into his lungs.

Natalie quickly stepped aside and delivered a blow to the side of Ryan's head that sent him reeling from the sheer power of her punch. As his head dropped, she threw a perfect uppercut to his jaw, striking him so hard that it broke two of her knuckles. Ryan's brain rattled in his skull, and then he fell to the floor unconscious. She shook her hand as the pain set in, and she knew that she had broken something.

Louhi had watched on in silence, and now she looked up at Natalie.

"Should I finish him off?" Natalie asked her. Louhi shook her head from side to side. "Take his phone. Call the police and tell them what he did to me and all the other girls he lied to. He will suffer the fate that he wanted for your husband. I have to go now. My time here is done." She said.

As Natalie took the phone from Ryan's pocket, Louhi walked back towards the painting, ready to make her way back to another realm.

"Can I ask you something before you go?" Natalie asked. Louhi stopped dead, but she did not turn around.

"You can ask me anything."

"Did my husband and you do anything that night?" There was a slight pause before she answered Natalie's question.

"No. Your husband showed me kindness and nothing more. Stay with him. Good men are hard to find these days." She replied, as she placed her hands back onto the canvas, the paint started to spread out from the centre of the painting. Slowly the picture that she had painted started to form again. She would be sealed within the void and would stay behind the painting forever.

It's alright

Natalie walked into the living room and unlocked Ryan's phone. Then she called the police telling them there was an intruder in her flat. She carried on into the kitchen and picked out a large knife from the block just in case Ryan woke up, but as she walked back out into the hallway, she saw that Ryan was no longer on the floor. He was gone. The front door was wide open and then she heard the communal door downstairs slam as it was closed.

She thought about giving chase and running after Ryan, but she soon thought better of it. The police would catch him soon enough, and more importantly, she now had all the evidence that she needed to set her husband free.

The police had arrived at the flat within minutes and Natalie handed over Ryan's mobile phone to the first officer who walked through the front door.

"My husband is innocent of murdering that girl. All the evidence that you need is stored here. Now get my husband out of prison before something bad happens to him there. Trust me, if he gets hurt, then we will be suing the police force."

"We will get forensics to go into the memory of the phone. It may take some time though. Please be patient..." The officer replied, but by this point, Natalie had heard enough.

"Fuck being patient! You aren't the one locked up for something you didn't do. Now get him out of there and do your fucking job properly this time!" She shouted angrily. The officer went red-faced, and he decided not to say anything else that might upset her further.

A taste of things to come

Gareth collected his items from the prison officer. He placed his watch on his right wrist and fastened the strap. He had lost weight in the few days that he had been inside, and his wrist was thinner than before. The watch felt loose, but it was still working and kept perfect time. He signed for his goods and then his escort took him out to the prison doors so that he could make his exit.

"Normally I tell the discharged inmates that I hope to never see them in here again. I don't think I need to say that to you. No hard feelings, eh?" The officer said, and he offered out his hand to Gareth.

"Go fuck yourself," Gareth replied and then he walked calmly out of the door to his freedom without looking back. He should never have been sent here in the first place, so he wasn't about to forgive them for his wrongful imprisonment. The short stay within the prison walls had damaged him in ways that he would not fully understand for months to come, but he knew that no one would ever do anything like this to him again.

He knew that his wife would be outside, and Natalie didn't disappoint him. As the scent of the world outside filled his nostrils, he sighed a huge sigh of relief. Natalie was standing next to her car, happily waiting to see her husband, and looking more beautiful than ever. The moment that she caught sight of Gareth, they smiled at each other, and she ran towards him. They held each other tightly, and for quite a long time, she held him close and refused to let him go.

Still breathing.

After spending some time in prison, it felt strange sleeping in a comfortable bed again. On his first night of freedom, Gareth took a long time to fall asleep, and when he finally succumbed to the tiredness, his dreams were dark. He awoke at around four in the morning, and his pillowcase was soaked with sweat. Natalie lay next to him, blissfully unaware of his nightmares.

It was just starting to become light outside, and he could see her face in the darkness. The time that they had spent apart had been torturous to him. His mind had played numerous tricks on him while they had been apart, and he was convinced that if he had been sentenced to a prison term, then Natalie would soon tire of waiting for him and eventually decide to move on.

Seeing Natalie's sleeping face catching the glow of the early morning light, made Gareth smile. He seldom appreciated how beautiful her face was without her make-up on. Her skin was smooth, and her lips supple. He had always loved her, but he had taken her for granted for far too long. Now that he was free, he was determined to make it up to her somehow. Gareth swung his legs over the side of the bed and stood up. His left knee cracked as he stretched his arms out wide. He put his dressing gown around his shoulders, placed his mobile phone in his pocket, and then he walked out to the bathroom.

As he lifted the toilet seat and he started to pee, he stared up at the loft hatch above him and his mind started to wander. Considering everything that had happened in the bathroom, Gareth could not help but recall the moment that he found the woman in the bath. He closed his eyes and shook his head to try and clear the image from his mind.

The woman was long dead and cremated, and yet he felt that he still had a connection to her. It felt like a part of her remained in the flat. Natalie had not mentioned anything to him about what had happened with the painting, strangely the thought of her spirit still being somewhere here within these walls was comforting to him. Then he felt a hand on his shoulder, and he jumped in fright.

Gareth turned to discover that it was only Natalie standing right behind him.

"You scared the shit out of me!" He told her. His face was flushed, and his breathing was heavy.

"I woke up, and you weren't there. I was worried about you." She started to kiss the back of his neck, while he shook the few remaining drops of urine away.

"Go back to bed. I will be joining you in just a few minutes."

Natalie playfully smacked Gareth on the backside, then she returned to the bedroom. Gareth felt sweaty, so he took his mobile out of his pocket, put his music on random play on a low volume and then he took off his dressing gown and ran a shower. The water was set at a low temperature, and as Gareth stepped into the flowing streams.

The water made him shiver until his body had adjusted to the temperature. A random artist named Lykke Li was playing in the background, and Gareth sang along to the words under his breath. Then an alert sounded on his phone. The alert was followed by another, and then another. Seven messages came through in all.

He turned off the shower and stepped out. Taking a towel from the shelf, he dried the top half of his body and then wrapped the towel around his waist. Gareth had assumed that the messages were from Natalie and that she must have heard him singing from the bedroom and was telling him how bad he sounded, but the messages were from an unknown number. He opened up the first one, and there was an image of his wife. She was naked in the picture. He walked out into the living room and opened up all of the messages one after the other. They became more and more explicit as he opened them.

Natalie felt a gentle pressure on her lips that woke her from her light sleep. Gareth was leaning over the bed, and she pulled him closer. She dragged him into the bed, where they made love for the first time in months. Gareth seemed to have changed since he had been in prison. He was no longer gentle with her. He was fucking her hard, and she was moaning with pleasure. She was making enough noise to disturb all the other flats in the block, but no one would complain. The sex was over quickly, but it was satisfying, and when he had finally finished, Gareth rolled over onto his side. He was facing away from his wife, and that was unusual for him.

Natalie ran her hand along Gareth's back. He had just taken a shower, but he was sweaty again. She didn't mind. She needed a shower too now.

"Shall we do something later today?" She suggested. She was thinking about going out to the beach or maybe taking him out for a meal somewhere nice.

"You can do something for me," Gareth told her

"What?" She smiled widely, hoping that it might lead to an exciting adventure.

"You can pack up your things and leave. I want you out of the flat, and I want a divorce." He replied.

Natalie slapped him gently on the shoulder and giggled.

"Come on, what is it that you want really?" Gareth turned around on the bed to face her. He took the wedding ring off of his finger and placed it in her hand.

"That was the last time that we will ever fuck. It was our last goodbye. Now get up, get out of my flat and get out of my life. I know what you did when you were away with Ryan. I saw everything."

A sense of dread washed over her as Natalie realised that Gareth knew about their affair. There was no point in trying to deny it. He always knew when she was lying to him.

"How do you know about us?" She asked, then she quickly tried to change tact "I'm so sorry Gareth, but if you let me explain…" She begged, but Gareth was having none of it.

"It's too late for that. I don't love you anymore. Goodbye." He said, pulling away. Those three lines convinced her that he meant what he was saying and that she would never change his mind.

Those exact words were lines from the film Closer, the film they had watched together while out on a first date. Natalie got out of bed and walked into the bathroom without saying another word. Her guilt was eating her up inside, and she was to blame for destroying the marriage. There was no way back once Gareth had made up his mind.

The bitter truth

Ryan had opened his eyes as he caught his breath. He was lucky to still be alive. He stumbled down the stairs and ran out of the block of flats. It was all over, and now he had no choice but to run. He had escaped from the country by speedboat with a little help from a few of his close associates. He had money hidden away for emergencies, and he could live a life of luxury, for as long as it took.

He was still angry about how Natalie had attacked and nearly killed him that day, and he wasn't finished with that woman yet, he still wanted to destroy her life in return for the injuries she had caused him. He used a spare phone to send the pictures and the videos to her husband that he had made in secret, including a video from the hotel in France. He hoped that Gareth would come to hate her for what she had done.

The final video that he sent to Gareth was one of his favourites. He never tired of hearing Natalie screaming out his name as she orgasmed. It was so satisfying for his ego. He was confident that these messages would have the desired effect, and he smiled as he pressed the send button for the final time. Then he turned off the phone and threw it in the bathroom bin in the hotel room.

He ran a bath, adding in luxurious amounts of rich bubbles, and when it was almost full to the brim, Ryan stepped inside of it. He placed his android phone on the shelf next to the bath and set the videos of himself and Natalie on a repeat cycle so that he could watch himself having sex with her repeatedly. As he slipped down into the hot water, he began to touch himself.

He closed his eyes as he listened to the pleasure in the sounds that Natalie made while he fucked her time after time, and he smiled to himself. Natalie may have beaten him in battle, but he had won the war in the end. In the bathroom mirror, a dark circle of black paint began to form, and Ryan had no idea about what was happening while he pleasured himself.

As he felt a sudden chill on his face and opened his eyes. He could not describe the horrific sight of the creature that was now balanced over his body. A decaying corpse of a woman on all fours resting on the rim of the bath, waiting for him. The moment that Ryan opened his mouth to shout out in terror, she fell on top of him with a force so tremendous, it that was heavy enough to weigh him down under the water.

The corpse of the woman held her open mouth over his as he screamed out for air, and maggots dropped from the cavities within her skull and down his throat. The moment when his lungs filled with water and he drowned, would come as a blessing.

Evanescent

The hotel manager had called the police and asked them to attend the hotel after a suspicious smell was found to be coming from one of the luxury rooms on the second floor. The hotel door was locked from the inside, and the staff had not been able to gain access to change the bedding or towels for the last three days. The officers had broken the door down and began to search the room.

It did not take long to discover the body of a man in the bathtub, lying still beneath the water, his eyes wide open in fear.

"Reminds me of Jim Morrison." One of the officers said.

"Fuck off. Don't you dare say shit like that! Don't be a jerk. Morrison was a genius, who died before his time. This guy looks like he was a pervert, he died with his cock in his hand. Looks like he was beating off to porn on his phone. More than likely gave himself a heart attack." The other officer replied.

"Did you notice his hair?"

"Yeah, he was probably trying to recapture his youth."

"If he died it blonde, I'd agree. His eyebrows are brown, but his hair is completely white."

"Maybe he's an albino, or maybe he saw a ghost?" The officer joked as he nudged his partner in the ribs playfully.

"Who the fuck knows. Better get him down to the morgue soon though. Then we got a lot of paperwork to fill in."

Both officers headed out into the hallway, while Ryan's corpse stared out from under the water. Behind the bathroom mirror, Ryan's spirit had been banging on the glass. He was trying his hardest to get the attention of the police officers. He could not accept that he was dead, and he was not prepared to move on to the next realm.

Louhi watched him desperately trying to find a way to make it back to the realm of the living, but she would never show him how it was possible. She pulled on the chains that she had fixed around his legs. Finally, the time had come, and she would drag his soul down to the depths of hell, to try and trade it with the devil for the release of her own tortured soul.

Printed in Great Britain
by Amazon